Shane

Susin Nielsen

James Lorimer & Company, Publishers
Toronto, 1989

1-55028-235-2 paper   1-55028-237-9 cloth

Canadian Cataloguing in Publication Data

Nielsen, Susin, 1964-
Shane
(Degrassi)

ISBN 1-55028-237-9 (bound) ISBN 1-55028-
235-2 (pbk.)

I. Title. II. Series.

PS8577.I45S49 1989   jC813'.54   C89-
094824-0
PZ7.N54Sh 1989

James Lorimer & Company, Publishers
Egerton Ryerson Memorial Building
35 Britain Street
Toronto, Ontario
M5A 1R7

This book is based on characters and stories from the television series *Degrassi Junior High*. The series was created by Linda Schuyler and Kit Hood for Playing With Time Inc., with Yan Moore as supervising writer.

Playing With Time Inc. acknowledges with thanks the writers whose enthusiasm and dedication helped produce the original scripts on which this story is based — Yan Moore, Avrum Jacobson, Susin Nielsen, Kathryn Ellis.

CHAPTER 1

Shane McKay pushed the peas around his plate with his fork. He hated peas and his mother knew it, but she insisted on serving them anyway because they were "good for him."

"Lovely weather today." His father's voice came from behind his newspaper.

"Mmhmm. Hard to believe it's the dead of winter," his mother replied, taking a moment away from the letter she was reading.

They sat at the dining room table, eating supper. Shane didn't know why they always had to eat in the dining room, with the fancy cutlery and plates, when it was just the three of them. But his parents had done it that way for as long as he could remember. They liked things to stay the same.

Shane ate his dinner in silence. He snuck

a look at his parents; they were both so involved in their reading, they didn't notice him studying their faces. His mom and dad often joked with each other that dinnertime was the only time they had to catch up on what was happening in the world.

Shane didn't like dinnertime. It was too quiet. Usually he would wolf down his meal and ask to be excused. But not tonight.

The old grandfather clock ticked away in the corner. As he listened to the steady "tick, tick, tick," he was sure it got louder. He shifted in his seat and cleared his throat, just to block out the sound for a second.

"Mrs. Carson called again today about her boy," his dad said to nobody in particular. His father was the minister at their community church, and he was always busy counselling members of his congregation.

"Oh, dear," said his mother. "I thought she might. I saw her at the Christian Women's Association meeting last night. She looked a wreck."

Shane wondered if that was a new group. His mother was on so many volunteer committees, he could never remember the names of them. Both his parents were admired greatly in the community, and Shane was very proud of them, but he sometimes wished they weren't involved in so many things. There wasn't a lot of time left over for him.

Mr. McKay put down his paper and looked at his son. Shane tried his best to look like nothing was bothering him.

"Tell me, Shane, do any of the kids in your school do drugs?"

Shane went to Degrassi Junior High, in the heart of downtown Toronto. When he had first started there in grade seven last year, he had been nervous about all the rumours he'd heard about drugs. But he'd never seen evidence of anything, not even pot.

"No. I don't think so."

"Have you ever heard of something called *crack* ?" His father pronounced it like it was a foreign word. Sometimes it amazed Shane that despite all their work in the community, his parents could still be so completely out of touch with the younger generation. Crack had been a topic of discussion for a long time.

But Shane had been taught never to be rude to his parents, so he answered politely, "Yeah."

"It's started to get into schools, apparently." His dad let out a heavy sigh. "I don't know, maybe I'm getting old, but it seems everywhere you turn these days, kids are messing themselves up one way or another."

Shane's heart started thumping so loud,

he was sure his parents could hear it. He quickly looked back down at his plate.

"It makes me appreciate what a fine young man you are, Shane," his father continued.

Shane shot a nervous glance at his dad. But Mr. McKay's expression was serene, and Shane knew he didn't suspect a thing.

His dad's comment about being old wasn't just one of those offhand remarks parents make. His mother and father *were* old. They were both in their mid-fifties. Shane had just turned fourteen.

Silence descended on the room again. Shane started to construct a face with the peas on his plate.

Mrs. McKay chuckled over something in her letter.

"What is it, dear?" asked his dad.

"That Carl," she replied. "He never ceases to amaze me. Straight A's in university!" She looked at Shane, grinning. "You can be proud of your older brother."

Shane smiled a forced grin and looked back down at his plate. Carl was six years older than he was. He hadn't lived at home for two years now, but Shane liked to think back on what it had been like when his brother still lived here. The house had been full of laughter, and dinner had been a time for lots of discussion and chatter. His parents

4

adored Carl. And now Carl was following in his father's footsteps, studying to become a minister.

"That's our boy," his dad replied proudly.

Shane remembered the day Carl had told their dad that he, too, wanted to become a minister. His dad hadn't stopped smiling for a whole week.

Shane tried hard to be like his older brother. He was on the basketball and soccer teams at school, just like Carl had been. He worked hard to get the best marks possible. He helped out with the Sunday School classes every week. He helped around the house and kept his own room spotless.

But no matter how hard he tried, he could never do quite as well as Carl. And perhaps because his parents assumed he would do as well as his brother, they never praised his achievements. They had produced one success already, and they expected the second one to be a success, too.

Shane had a lot of theories about his parents. For instance, he believed that his parents never dreamed they'd have a teenaged boy in their home at this point in their lives. He was positive he was a "mistake." His parents had never told him that, but he only had to look at the facts. There was a six-year age difference between him and Carl. His parents were old.

Because of their religion, they would have never dreamed of not having him, but he hadn't been born out of love like Carl. He had been born out of a bad judgement call. At least, that was Shane's theory.

Suddenly Shane looked up to see his mom eyeing him disapprovingly. "Don't you think it's about time you got a haircut?" she asked. Shane's hair was short blond, far from long. "I can see it curling over a bit at the back."

"Sure, okay." Shane hated arguments. He took after his parents in that way; he didn't like to rock the boat. But it was comments like this that made him realize just how old and set in their ways his parents were.

It was weird sometimes, having old parents. When other kids joked about the generation gap, he knew exactly what they meant. Last year at parents' night, one of the kids had asked if they were his grandparents. He had felt embarrassed, not for himself but for his mom and dad.

"The situation in the Middle East just never gets better," said his dad, not looking up from the paper. "So much turmoil."

"We can be thankful we live in such a peaceful place," his mom clucked.

Shane shot a look at his mother, then looked back down at the face he was creating on his plate. He only had to do the mouth. He turned the peas downward into a frown.

For most of his life, he hadn't had to keep secrets from his parents, because he never did anything wrong. But since he started grade eight six months ago, he felt there were so many things he couldn't tell them. In the past few months, he had kept more secrets from them than he had in his entire life.

The grandfather clock was driving him crazy. He felt like he was about to burst. He hadn't touched his food because he knew his stomach wouldn't keep it down.

All he had ever wanted was to be accepted, by his parents and the kids at school. He didn't want to be a star football player. He knew he wouldn't find the cure for cancer. He didn't want to become prime minister. He just wanted people to like him. He just wanted to fit in.

He felt he had been on the right track, too. Until now.

CHAPTER 2

It had all started when he began dating Spike. Her real name was Christine, but everyone called her Spike because of her wild hair, which she did every morning so it would stick straight up. She was popular and pretty. Shane couldn't believe she would ever notice him. But she did.

Shane had always been a loner. Sometimes he daydreamed about being friends with Joey Jeremiah, or Derek Wheeler, the guy everyone called Wheels. Shane thought that was great, having a nickname. Joey and Wheels were two of the coolest guys in school. They had no problems talking to anyone, even the best-looking girls. But Shane could barely talk to other guys, let alone the girls.

He was taller than most of the boys in

grade eight. He had blond hair and blue eyes. Some of his relatives told him he was handsome, but he didn't believe them; after all, relatives always said that stuff. But when he heard through the school grapevine that Spike thought he was cute, well ...

That was about five months ago, in September. Shane was out on the soccer field practising his footwork. He had practised a lot over the summer, and he was determined to make the team this year. He saw his friend, Wai-Lee, approaching him.

Shane still felt bad about Wai-Lee. He had kind of dumped him when he started hanging around Spike's friends. Wai-Lee was really nice and really smart but, like Shane, he wasn't exactly popular. The two of them would often go downtown together on weekends and check out the latest video games. But when Shane got the chance to hang out with the popular crowd, he went for it.

Shane remembered how he had started goofing around, bouncing the soccer ball off his head when he saw Wai-Lee coming his way. But Wai-Lee's mind was on other things.

"Boy, did I just hear the wildest piece of gossip."

Shane kept bouncing the ball with his

head. "Yeah? What?"

His friend reached up and grabbed the ball in mid-air. "I was in the library," Wai-Lee continued in a conspirational tone, "and Spike and Heather and Erica were at the table next to me." (Heather and Erica were twins, and they were Spike's best friends.) "They were talking about boys, and your heartthrob, Spike —"

"She's not my heartthrob!" Shane retorted hotly.

"Right," Wai-Lee smirked. "You only practically drool when she walks past."

"I do not!" Shane glanced around to make sure nobody could hear them.

"Then how come you're red as a beet?"

"Cause I've been working out, that's why," Shane mumbled.

"Anyway, let me finish! Spike leaned over to Heather and Erica and said, 'I think Shane is the cutest guy at Degrassi.'" Wai-Lee smiled, triumphant.

When Shane walked home later that day, he thought he was floating. After that, he and Spike started smiling shyly at each other in the halls. Then they graduated to saying hi. Then, at one of the school dances, he got up the nerve to ask her to dance.They danced all night and at the end of the dance, they walked outside holding hands.

"Spike?" he started, trying to hide the waver in his voice, "would you ... gosteadywithme?" Right after he blurted it out he wished he hadn't. He wasn't even sure if people went steady in the eighties. He'd only seen it done on old reruns of "Happy Days." He lowered his head.

"Yes," was her unexpected reply. She smiled shyly at him. Shane felt glued to the spot. He didn't know what to say next. But there was no need for words. Spike stood on tiptoe and kissed him. Shane felt himself unglue, and he leaned over and kissed her back. His first real kiss.

Even after they had been dating for a while, he still had to pinch himself to make sure it wasn't a dream. After all, they didn't have much in common. She wore a black leather jacket and pointy black boots, and she knew all the latest music. Shane wore the button-down shirts and topsiders that his mother bought him, and he didn't have a clue what was happening on the music scene. He was in awe of Spike. He thought she was absolutely beautiful.

It was around that time that he kind of dumped Wai-Lee. Wai-Lee would call him up on Saturdays like he always did and ask if he wanted to go downtown. But now Shane said no, until finally Wai-Lee stopped phoning. Eventually, Shane didn't even say hello to him in the halls. Looking back, he felt like an idiot. He would do anything for a friend like Wai-Lee now. But Wai-Lee had moved to Montreal over Christmas, so Shane was on his own.

He was surprised to discover that Spike was almost as shy as he was when it came to dating. They went to lots of movies so they wouldn't have to try to make conversation all night. They would sit in the back row of the theatre and hold hands. Sometimes they would neck. And one night, in a little park by Spike's house, she let him lie down on top of her, and he put his hand up her shirt. It only lasted a moment, before she pulled his hand away and stood up; but Shane savoured the sensation. He had never felt that way before.

Going out with Spike had other benefits as well. Some of the other popular kids started saying hi to him in the halls. Then in November, something really great happened.

He was sitting at his desk before class when two soft hands covered his eyes.

"Hey, Shane. Guess who." He turned around and smiled at Spike, grabbing her hands and holding them.

"What are you doing this Saturday night?" she asked.

"Nothing."

"Lucy's having a party and we're invited. Wanna go?"

Did he want to go?!! He remained collected. "Uh ... sure."

Spike smiled and moved to her own seat. The bell rang and Mr. Raditch, their teacher, began a lesson. But Shane didn't hear a word.

Lucy was *the* party girl at Degrassi, and getting invited to one of her parties meant she considered him part of the "in" crowd. Shane knew the invitation was extended to him only because he was seeing Spike, but so what? He would show them he could fit in.

He didn't tell his parents about the party. In fact, he didn't even tell them about Spike. He hated lying, but it wasn't worth the trouble it would have caused. His parents would only tell him he was too young to date and that he should be concentrating on his studies. Or, worse, they would want to meet her. Shane could just picture it. One look at Spike and his parents would forbid him to see her.

So, on the night of the party he told his parents he was meeting friends downtown. He was sure they could see right through him, because he couldn't keep from blushing whenever he fibbed. But they didn't even notice, probably because they'd never dream he would lie to them.

"Just be careful," his mom said. "We don't want you getting into any trouble."

So Shane went off to the party. And boy, did he get into trouble. At the time, though, he was sure it was the best night of his life.

Because that night, Shane McKay lost his virginity.

He could barely remember how it happened. They had both seemed drunk with excitement, and when Shane pulled Spike into one of the bedrooms, she let him. They didn't say a word to each other. One thing led to another ....

Then he was inside her. It was an incredible, weird feeling. He had no self-control, and it was over within seconds, but at the time that didn't matter. What mattered was he'd done it!

The next morning at breakfast, when his parents asked him about his "evening downtown with the boys," and he answered their questions with more fibs, he felt guilty and ashamed, thinking how one lie always led to another.

If they knew the truth, he was certain they would kill him, or at least disown him. But as he washed the breakfast dishes, he started to relax. His parents would never have to know, and what they didn't know wouldn't hurt them.

At school over the next couple of weeks, he was the topic of a lot of speculation. Even Joey and Wheels talked to him, cornering him in the bathroom at school one day.

Shane was combing his hair when they came in. Joey was never one to skirt around an issue, so he came right out and said it.

"Hey, man, what really happened at Lucy's party? What were you doing in the bedroom?"

Shane looked at Joey's reflection in the mirror, grinning slyly, and said in the coolest voice he could muster, "Wouldn't you like to know."

Joey and Wheels looked at each other, then back at Shane.

"If you really did it," Joey continued, "tell us what it was like."

Shane wanted to milk this for all it was worth. He had already decided he wasn't going to tell ... but he wasn't exactly *not* going to tell, either. He knew that wasn't very nice, but he really wanted Joey and Wheels to like him.

"Why?" he replied. "You guys never had sex?"

"Yeah," Joey said quickly. "Of course I've had sex!"

"Me, too," Wheels said. "Lots of times."

Joey gave Shane an impatient punch on the arm. "So tell us! Did you, or did you not, do it?"

Shane turned and looked at Joey. "None of your business," he grinned broadly.

Wheels changed tactics. "How come Spike won't talk to you anymore?"

Shane quickly turned his back on the boys and wet his comb in the sink. Wheels was right. Spike had been avoiding him like he was carrying some deadly disease, ever since the party.

"She's in a bad mood, I guess," he mumbled, shrugging his shoulders.

"Probably her period or something," Joey joked as they left the bathroom.

Shane wished Joey had been right.

CHAPTER 3

Finally he found out why Spike had been avoiding him. He confronted her in the hall one day. She tried to move away from him, but he stood right in front of her.

"Wait! I thought we were going steady," he said. "Why are you treating me like this?"

Spike looked him square in the eye. There was a strange mixture of sadness and disgust in her eyes. "You really want to know?"

"Yes." Sometimes Shane wished he had never said yes. Sometimes he wished he had just walked away and never talked to her again, because in one sentence, the life he had felt was turning into one big dream turned into one big nightmare.

"I think I'm pregnant."

And she was.

Now Shane was about to do what he should have done almost two months ago. He picked up his fork and pressed down on his peas, watching the fleshy insides squirt out, making the frown look more like a grimace. He took a deep breath.

"Mom ... Dad ...? There's something I've got to tell you."

CHAPTER 4

When Shane finally looked up from his plate, he felt like a nuclear bomb had just dropped and that he was the one who had pushed the button. Now he had to survey the damage.

His father's face was white. His mother looked like she was going to burst into tears. Shane waited for one of them to say something. And waited. He shifted in his seat.

Finally Mr. McKay spoke in a slow, shaky voice. "How could you do this to us?" Shane saw that his father was clenching his fists and his knuckles were white.

"I didn't mean to do anything to hurt you," Shane mumbled, lowering his head again.

"You're fourteen!" said his mother. "How could you even *think* of having sex?"

"We didn't really think," admitted Shane.

"Well, that's obvious!" his father replied. "Have you forgotten everything we've taught you? Has it all gone in one ear and out the other?"

"No! It … just happened."

"What kind of girl would let this happen?" said his dad.

"It wasn't her fault. It was just a dumb mistake." Even though Spike hated him now, Shane had made up his mind to defend her.

"A dumb mistake?" His dad's voice rose for the first time. "Do you realize what this means, for all of us?"

Shane sank further down into his seat. He felt like he was physically shrinking in size. Maybe he would just keep shrinking till he disappeared. It didn't seem like such a bad idea.

"What is she going to do?" his mom asked suddenly.

"She's going to have it. Then put it up for adoption, I guess." He realized as he said it that he and Spike had never really discussed what she would do when the baby was born.

"Well, I guess we can be grateful for that." Mr. and Mrs. McKay didn't believe in abortion. But if Spike had had an abortion, he thought, he would never have had to tell his parents. He quickly pushed the thought from his head.

"What will I tell the members of the congregation?" His dad put his head in his hands and rubbed his forehead. He looked tired. Shane stared at his father's balding, white-haired head, his stomach full of knots again.

"Do you have to tell them?" he asked timidly.

"Shane," his father said, trying to control his mounting anger, "do you realize how many people in the congregation have children who go to Degrassi? What will they think? The minister's son ..."

"What did we do wrong?" his mom's voice cracked. "We tried to bring you up in a good, religious environment."

"I can't believe we didn't see something like this coming," his dad said sadly. "How could you deceive us like this?"

"I didn't mean to deceive you. I just didn't want to worry you."

His father snorted. "Well, it certainly backfired, young man."

Silence descended on the room again. Shane knew it wasn't only the shame that was making his parents so upset. It was the fact that, in their eyes, he had sinned. He saw a tear run down his mother's face.

His mind was racing. "I could marry her," he blurted out. He watched his father's face turn from white to bright red.

"Don't be ridiculous!" His dad was shouting for the first time. "You've caused enough trouble already." He looked away from his son, and Shane realized his dad couldn't even look him in the eye, he was so ashamed of him. "Go to your room," Mr. McKay said quietly.

"I'm sorry. I'm really sorry." He didn't want to go upstairs, not yet. He wanted to run over to his mother and have her hold him close and tell him everything would be okay, like she used to do when he was younger. But he stayed put.

"Go to your room," his dad repeated. "Now."

Shane rose from the dinner table. His food was cold and untouched. He walked out of the room, feeling his parents' anger burning into him.

In his bedroom, everything was neat and tidy. There were no posters on the walls, because his parents didn't like that kind of thing. Shane had always tried to abide by their rules. Now he had made one big, dumb mistake, and he felt like it would prey on him for the rest of his life.

He lay down on his bed and stared at the ceiling. If he leaned back far enough, he could see the cross that hung above his bed.

He reached up and took it down. Turning it over, he saw the inscription on the back: "To Carl, with love, Mom and Dad." Shane always got Carl's hand-me-downs. Even the cross was a hand-me-down. He stared at it for a moment, then put it under his bed.

He wished Wai-Lee hadn't moved. Nobody at school would talk to him anymore, because they thought he was a big jerk.

Downstairs, he could hear his parents talking in low voices. He heard his mother start to cry. Shane closed his eyes and put his pillow over his head to block out the sound. Then he started to sob, but no tears came — just sharp, uncontrollable shaking.

CHAPTER 5

Shane dragged his feet up the front walk of Degrassi the next day with his head lowered. Ever since the kids at school had found out Spike was pregnant, he had walked with his head down, staring at the pavement.

It wasn't that the kids judged him or Spike. There were the expected few who did, but a lot of the students were very supportive of Spike. Most of them were far nicer to Spike than they were to him. Shane knew he hadn't exactly been helpful when Spike told him she was pregnant; in fact, he had ignored her for weeks. Most of the kids believed it was his problem, too, and that he should be there for Spike. Shane thought it was easy for them to say that; they weren't in his shoes.

Now he wanted to change. It had taken a lot of guts to tell his parents, and he knew he would be facing the consequences for a long time. But at least he could tell himself he had done the right thing for a change.

Now he wanted to help Spike, too.

The night before, he had started to think about the fact that Spike was really going to have a baby. His baby. Their baby. And he remembered his mother's question about what Spike was going to do with the baby. He had always assumed she was going to put it up for adoption, but maybe she wouldn't. Maybe she would keep it. Tossing and turning in bed, Shane had imagined what it would be like to have a real baby, and somehow it didn't seem all that bad. A baby wouldn't be disappointed in him. A baby might even look up to him.

Going toward the front steps, he heard "Hi, Daddy." It was Kathleen, a nasty grade seven girl who was sitting on the steps. Shane gave her an evil look and kept walking. He couldn't believe it! Even the seventh graders were ganging up on him.

In a way it was funny how he had always wanted to be the centre of attention. Now, everywhere he went at school he was the centre of attention, and he hated it. He wished he could just slip back into the old days.

Eyes followed him as he walked down the hall. Even though there was lots of chatter coming from the students milling about in the corridor, it always seemed to become unusually quiet when he passed by.

He found Spike at her locker and approached her warily. Lately all she did was yell at him the moment he came near her.

"Hi," he said hesitantly. Spike turned around, and Shane had to remind himself not to look at her belly. She wasn't getting big yet, but he knew she was sensitive about it. So he forced himself to look into her cold, green eyes. She was eating a bag of chips and sipping on a pop. She just stared at him.

"I told them," Shane said.

Spike looked surprised. "You told your parents about the baby?!" Shane knew she had given up any hope that he might tell his parents. "What did they say?"

"They were upset. But they didn't yell and scream and stuff." Shane had decided the night before that he wouldn't tell her just how upset his parents had been. After all, she had more than enough troubles of her own.

"Well," she said, smiling, "that's good." Shane wanted to throw his arms around her and hug her. It had been a long time since she had smiled at him. It had been a long time since anyone had smiled at him.

"They want us to get together," he started. Before he'd left the house that morning, his father had come out of his study and told him to arrange a meeting. He had also told Shane they would have a long talk when he got home. Then he had walked out of the kitchen and shut himself in his study again. Now Shane had the whole day to sweat about this "long talk."

"They want us to talk. You, me, them and your mom."

Spike's face fell. "Oh, no, that's horrible!"

"I know."

"What are we going to do?" Spike really looked worried, and Shane was pleased that she was asking him for advice, even though he couldn't give her any.

"I don't know," he shrugged. Spike closed her locker and they started to walk to class. Shane noticed that Heather and Erica were watching them with interest. It had been a long time since they had walked to class together.

Shane took a deep breath. "Uh ... Spike? I was thinking a lot last night about everything ..." Spike just looked at him. "Do you ever think about keeping the baby?"

Spike's eyes opened wide. "What?"

"Seriously," Shane continued quickly, "wouldn't it be neat to have a little baby who loved you? And respected you, and needed you?"

Spike was looking at him like he was crazy. "Shane, I'm a kid," she replied. "Not somebody's mother."

He shut up. He didn't want to ruin the moment. It was nice they were getting along for a change. Spike took another swig of pop and stuck her hand into her potato chip bag.

He touched her arm gently. "You shouldn't eat that stuff," he said before he could stop himself. "It's bad for the baby."

Spike knocked his hand away angrily. "Mind your own business."

"It *is* my business," he said hotly. "It's my baby, too."

"Right!" said Spike, loud enough that a few heads turned. "It's so easy for you boys. You don't have to get fat. You don't have to go to counselling. You don't have to be responsible." She disappeared into the class-room.

"I'm *trying* to be responsible!" he yelled after her.

He realized the halls were quiet. He looked around at the faces staring at him. Lowering his head again, he walked into class.

CHAPTER 6

Shane opened the front door to his house. It was a beautiful old house, comfortable and warm. Until today, he had always been happy to come home after school.

His father was on the phone and didn't hear him come in. "That's wonderful, Carl. Congratulations. We're very proud of you. Top marks in your classes!"

Shane wanted to run in and ask if he could talk to his brother. Carl had always been good at listening to him when he was still at home, and he really needed someone to listen to him now.

His father continued. "If only Shane were more like you."

Shane froze in the doorway. He felt like he had just been slapped in the face.

"Oh, your mother and I are fine, I suppose.

We're just very upset with your brother. It's such a mess, getting that girl pregnant. Mother's heartbroken. She daren't face her bridge club tonight. It's all very embarrassing."

Shane felt his face grow hot. He was fourteen years old and terrified, and all his mother could worry about was her dumb bridge club.

"… your mother and I reached a decision today. We're sending him to private school …"

Shane clutched one of the hooks on the coat rack. He suddenly had the sensation that he was about to collapse, like a carefully constructed house of cards that had just been hit by a gust of wind.

"… Strathcona, of course. After all, you went there."

Shane couldn't listen to another word. He slammed the door and walked into the kitchen. His mother was at the table, dabbing her eyes. His father looked up.

"… I have to go, Carl. Shane's home. We'll call you tomorrow … all right. We love you. Bye."

We love you. Shane had never heard his parents say that to *him*.

His mother and father looked at him, then at each other.

Finally, Shane spoke. He didn't want to get into an argument, but after all that had happened the day before, maybe one more argument didn't make much difference. His voice was shaking. "I don't want to go to private school. I like Degrassi."

"That doesn't mean you won't like Strathcona. Your brother went there and he enjoyed it," his father said, rubbing his forehead.

"I'm not like him," Shane mumbled.

"Well, maybe it's time you started trying to be," said Mr. McKay, his voice rising. Shane winced. He stood by the doorway, silent.

"Come now, Shane," his mother said. "It'll be good for you to get away. You'll be able to concentrate on your studies."

"But I want to be here to help when the baby's born."

"When the baby's born, it's going straight up for adoption. You're not even going to see it," his dad said firmly.

Shane looked at him. "What if it doesn't go up for adoption?"

His mother started to cough uncontrollably. Shane wasn't sure what was happening to him. It was like he was baiting them, purposely trying to get into a fight. But he was confused, and he wanted to talk.

His father was not in the mood for a discussion. He looked right back at his son, and said in a low, even voice, "Now, you listen to me, young man. You've done quite enough damage already."

"But I don't *want* to go to private school," Shane whined, realizing he sounded like a little kid. Things might not be great for him at Degrassi, but it had to be better than private school. Strathcona was located in a small town a few hours east of Toronto.

Private school meant uniforms, strict rules and religion classes. And all boys. No girls within miles. No wonder his parents wanted him to go there. It sounded like prison.

And he didn't want to live away from his parents. He liked his home. He didn't want to live with a bunch of strangers. He needed his parents, but how could he tell them that? It would be far too embarrassing. After all, he told himself, he was fourteen.

Besides, he had made up his mind he was going to be around to help Spike, any way he could.

But his dad wouldn't be moved. "End of discussion, Shane."

"But — "

"End of discussion."

Shane got up slowly from his chair. It felt

32

like a *déjà vu* from the night before. He started to leave the kitchen and, turning at the doorway, he saw his father lower his head and slowly shake it back and forth.

His parents were trying to get rid of him. He had disgraced them and instead of being there for him, they wanted to send him into exile. For the first time in his life, he hated his parents.

It surprised Shane to realize this. He had heard that there was a fine line between love and hate, and he guessed that was how he felt. He loved his parents more than anyone else in the world, but he hated them for shutting him out.

Everybody — Spike, his parents, even the kids at school — thought he was an irresponsible idiot. He wished he could prove to them that they were wrong.

CHAPTER 7

During the next few weeks, Shane felt like a stranger in his own home. He stayed at school as late as possible every afternoon, then slowly walked home, dreading the moment he arrived. The three of them ate dinner in silence, except for the occasional remark his father would make to his mom about something he had read in the paper. They seldom said a word to him. Shane thought they looked older than ever.

He didn't dare tell his parents that he needed their help. He only had to look at their faces to see how much they were suffering, and he figured the best thing he could do right now was to keep his mouth shut.

So he didn't bring up private school. He knew his parents had sent away for all the necessary forms, and he knew they had made many phone calls to Strathcona. It wasn't easy to get someone enrolled over halfway through the school year but, because Carl had gone there, it seemed that his parents were going to get their way.

His mom cried a lot. Shane caught her occasionally, as she sat knitting. A few times he tried to comfort her, but she brushed him off. He felt like a murderer trying to comfort the mother of the person he had just killed.

Often Shane would hear his father speaking in a low voice on the phone, to different members of the congregation. He knew how difficult it was for his father to tell them about his son. He did it one day in church. He asked Shane to stay at home that day. It was only the second time in his life he could remember missing church, and the first time was because he was sick with measles.

His father felt a strong moral obligation to the people who attended his church, and he preferred to tell them himself about Shane rather than have them hear about it through the grapevine. Besides, he had heard hundreds of personal woes and dilemmas from his congregation, so it only seemed right.

Shane found out later that there had actually been talk of making his dad step down. Fortunately the people came to their senses and realized it would be a stupid mistake on their part. His dad was the best minister the church had ever seen. But they weren't so easy on Shane. They decided he should no longer be helping out with the Sunday School classes. He supposed they thought he would be a bad influence just by being there.

Usually Shane didn't mind going to church, but now he hated it. People stared at him, and he kept thinking that the quotes his dad used were directed at him.

He wasn't even sure any more if he was religious. This was something he would never tell his parents in a million years. But he was having such a hard time believing in himself these days, he just couldn't figure out how he could believe in God.

CHAPTER 8

It was taking much too long to arrange a dinner date with Spike and her mom. Shane kept bugging Spike about it, and Spike kept telling him her mom said no every time she asked. Finally, Shane asked his father to call Ms. Nelson. Though part of him dreaded it, he really wanted them to have this meeting.

Now he sat at the kitchen table with his mom, pretending to read his history notes while his dad called Spike's mother. His mom was knitting a baby sweater for a woman in the church who was expecting.

The call only took a minute. "Okay, fine. That's fine ... see you then." His dad hung up, then he studied his son for a moment. "Shane, you did tell Spike that we wanted to have this dinner meeting, didn't you?"

"Of course! About ten times."

"Well, Spike mustn't have told her mother, then. Ms. Nelson told me this is the first she's heard of it."

"Somehow, that doesn't surprise me," Mrs. McKay piped up.

"What's that supposed to mean?" Shane challenged her.

"Any girl who would allow herself to get pregnant at that age, can't be reliable."

"That's not fair, Mom. She's just scared. Like me."

"She's got good reason to be scared. I'm surprised she even told her mother."

"Unlike some kids, Spike is very close to her mom." Shane waited for the dig to sink in, but they didn't even notice.

"Spike. What kind of a name is that for a girl anyway?" His mother was getting upset now.

"Her real name's Christine," Shane answered gently. "Everyone calls her Spike because of her hair."

"So she's a punk rocker!" Tears were welling up in his mother's eyes. Shane sighed and rolled his eyes.

"At any rate," his father said, getting them back on topic, "we're to meet with them tomorrow night. At the Porthouse restaurant."

Mrs. McKay looked up from her knitting.

"A restaurant? I was thinking I could cook a roast and we could have them over here."

Mr. McKay shrugged. "She insisted on a restaurant."

Shane smiled to himself. He was glad the meeting was arranged. This would give him the chance to prove he was a responsible, caring young man.

The next day at school, Shane went up to Spike after English class. Her stomach seemed to get larger every day.

"You nervous about tonight?"

"Yeah! Why did your dad have to call?"

"Well, you know, he's a minister and everything." He left out the fact that he had asked his dad to call. Spike probably would have punched him in the stomach.

Spike sighed, and Shane noticed her bottom lip quiver a bit, like she might cry. It seemed to him that a lot of people were crying these days.

"Don't worry," he reassured her. "We won't let 'em push us around."

Suddenly Spike smiled at him. "I've got to get to math. See you tonight."

Shane watched her walk down the hall. He still couldn't believe that the baby growing in her stomach was part of him, too.

CHAPTER 9

Shane sat with his parents at a large table in the Porthouse restaurant. It was a family restaurant, with reasonable prices, reasonable food and reasonable decor. Shane hoped they would have a reasonable meeting.

It had taken him close to half an hour to decide what to wear. He had finally decided on his light pink sweater and dress pants, because it was his mom's favourite outfit. She always told him he looked like such a fine young man when he wore it.

His mother fiddled with her cutlery, then straightened her napkin. They hardly ever ate in restaurants because she thought it was a waste of money.

"I don't see why we had to come here," she said tensely. "I could have cooked a perfectly good meal at home." But Shane could understand Ms. Nelson's decision to hold this meeting on neutral ground. If he had been in her shoes, he would have done the same thing.

"I'm sure this will be fine," Mr. McKay reassured her.

Shane looked at his watch and shifted in his seat. Spike and her mom should have arrived ten minutes ago. He hoped they were going to show up. He glanced toward the entrance.

"Here they are," he said, realizing he had almost shouted. His heart leapt as he waved them over. Ms. Nelson had her arm around her daughter.

Shane stared at Spike as they got closer. He wished he could be the one with his arm around her, making her feel safe.

Spike was wearing a CULT T-shirt and a short skirt. On her feet were her pointy black boots. Shane admired her for choosing to be herself, even for this uncomfortable occasion. He looked down at his own clothes, suddenly wondering if he had made the right choice. But he had never made any personal statements through his clothes.

He caught the momentary surprise on his parents' faces when they saw Spike. But they were equally surprised by Spike's mom. She was really young. He remembered Spike telling him once that her mom had become pregnant with her when she was seventeen. Spike had been a mistake, just like Shane. He thought ruefully that they should have learned something from it; instead, they had got together and created their own mistake.

Mr. McKay rose from his seat. Shane could see his mother's eyes rest disapprovingly on Spike's hair, then on her growing stomach.

His father spoke. "Ms. Nelson? I'm Steven McKay." It sounded weird when his father used his first name. He just seemed like a "Mister."

"How do you do," replied Spike's mom.

"This is my wife, Mary."

"How do you do," his mother said tersely. Shane wished they would cut the formalities and sit down. His father was trying too hard to be polite. And he could hear the tone in his mother's voice, which he felt was verging on rude.

"And you must be Spike," said his dad.

Spike didn't say anything. "Her name's Christine," her mom said firmly.

There was a moment of uneasy silence. "Yes, yes, of course," said his father quickly. "Christine."

Shane tried to catch Spike's eye, to tell her through his look that everything would be okay. But she wouldn't look at him. His dad motioned to two chairs across the table.

"Won't you sit down?" Finally, thought Shane. Now they could get on with things. The waiter approached the table.

"Would you like a drink?" Shane's dad asked Ms. Nelson.

"Thank you," she replied, looking not at Mr. McKay but at the waiter. "I'll have a Bailey's on ice. And can you put that on a separate cheque, please."

There was an uncomfortable silence as the waiter walked away. Shane sure could see where Spike had got her stubborn streak. He realized he was playing with the salt shaker. He stopped immediately, and sat on his hands.

The silence continued, becoming increasingly uncomfortable. Again he tried to catch Spike's eye, but she was staring resolutely at the tablecloth. Mr. McKay cleared his throat to signal that the lecture was about to begin. Shane only hoped his father wouldn't say anything embarrassing.

"You know, Ms. Nelson," his dad began, "as a minister I have professional experience in matters like this."

Shane couldn't help but think that if his dad was so experienced, then how come he couldn't help his own son?

His father continued. "What's happened

has happened. No point getting into all of that. We have to live in the present." He paused for a breath. "Now, in situations like this, emotions tend to run high. I know it's never easy. But I'm sure we're all going to handle this very reasonably."

Shane slouched back in his seat. He didn't know it yet, but the evening was going to be far from reasonable.

Their meals arrived and everyone started eating in silence. The conversation so far had been sparse and tense, a clash of two very strong, very different wills.

He could only pretend to eat. He noticed that Spike was doing the same thing, pushing the food around her plate with her fork. Her mom kept patting her knee. Shane suddenly envied the two of them. They were so close!

"Good food," said his father. Nobody responded, except his mother, who seemed to make a snorting sound under her breath. Shane couldn't help but feel sorry for his dad. He knew that in his own old-fashioned way, he really was just trying to help.

The waiter came by and refilled Ms. Nelson's glass. Again Shane caught his mother's disapproving glance. His parents didn't touch alcohol.

"Now, if you'd like," his father tried again,

"I can recommend a good home where your daughter can stay until afterward."

Spike's fork dropped with a clatter. She turned to her mom, frightened. "I don't want to go away!" Shane thought that was exactly how he had sounded when his parents had announced they were sending him to boarding school. He realized they really liked the idea of exile.

But, unlike his parents, Spike's mom listened. "You're not going to," she said, putting her arm around her daughter. She looked Mr. McKay right in the eye. "Christine is staying with me."

"Ms. Nelson," his dad said soothingly, "it's sometimes in the young person's best interests to get away. People can be very cruel."

Shane felt like covering his ears. His dad didn't know what was in Spike's best interests, or in Shane's best interests. He was just trying to sweep the problem under a carpet by getting both him and Spike out of town.

"And sometimes it's in the young person's best interests to stay at home," Ms. Nelson replied curtly. "I'm not going to send her away like she's committed a crime."

Shane looked at his father, who was silent. He knew that his parents did view this entire situation as a crime, and they thought the culprits should be punished.

He wondered if he would ever get a chance to speak. It didn't seem like the adults wanted to hear from either him or Spike.

His dad tried to brighten his tone. "Well, I'm happy that Shane's agreed to go away to private school."

That was the final straw. All night they had been talking about him and Spike like they weren't even there.

"No, I haven't," he blurted out. He could feel everyone's eyes on him.

"We've been through all this," his father said, in a tone that meant they should discuss it later, in private. But Shane wasn't about to stop now.

"But you never listen to me!" He realized his voice was getting louder, but he didn't care. Now that he had started, he wanted to announce his plan. "Dad, you've always taught me to do what's right. That's what I'm trying to do."

All night his father had been controlling his own anger, but now he spoke with force. "Getting her pregnant certainly proved that, didn't it?" People at the neighbouring tables suddenly stopped talking. Spike stared down at the tablecloth, mortified. His father lowered his voice.

"Look, son, we're only trying to do what's best for you."

"No, you're not!" Shane retorted. "You're trying to do what's best for *you*! You want me to go away because I embarrass you. So Mom can play bridge again." Everything he had kept hidden inside for the past few weeks came spilling out. He was on the verge of tears. He knew the other diners were watching the drama at their table unfold, but he didn't care anymore. "Sorry I'm not perfect like Carl."

"No one said that," his father said quietly.

"But that's what you *think*. I know I made a mistake. But give me a chance ... let me keep the baby."

Everyone's cutlery dropped on cue. They all looked at him like he was absolutely crazy. Even Spike.

"Let me show you ... you'll be proud of me." Shane's voice trailed off as he looked around the table at the incredulous stares he was getting. He tried to meet their eyes with a determined look, but his gaze wavered.

Suddenly, Spike's mom stood up and reached for her purse. She tossed some money on the table.

"Thank you so much for the invitation," she said coldly. "It doesn't appear we have much to talk about right now. May I suggest, Reverend McKay, that you listen to your own family and solve your own problems before

47

offering to solve ours ..."

Shane watched Spike leave the restaurant with her mom. Then he jumped up from the table and ran out the door, leaving his parents staring at their unfinished dinners.

He had expected to walk out of the restaurant feeling great. He had expected to walk out of the restaurant feeling accepted again. Instead, he was running out as fast as he could, feeling like a big jerk.

CHAPTER 10

"Okay, you can stay at Degrassi," Mr. McKay sighed. Shane glanced up at his dad, then quickly lowered his head again. He knew his eyes were puffy and red. He couldn't remember when he had cried so much.

When he had left the restaurant, he hadn't gone home immediately. The restaurant was a good five miles from their house, and Shane had walked home, crying the whole way. He hated crying. Even though he knew it was okay for boys to cry, it still made him feel like a baby.

When he had seen his parents' Plymouth Reliant parked outside the house, he almost hadn't gone in. For a moment he had thought wildly that he could run away. But he had no money and no clothes. He wished he could go to a friend's place for a few days and just hide out, so his parents would really worry about him, but he didn't have any friends he could turn to. As he had stood there, staring at the house, he had the horrible sensation that he was the only person on earth.

He had gone inside.

When he walked in, his parents didn't even look up. They sat in separate armchairs in the living room — not reading, not talking, just sitting. Shane could see the worry lines in his mother's face. She looked worn out.

And now his dad was agreeing to let him stay at Degrassi. But it didn't feel like a triumph for Shane. His dad wasn't doing it because he had all of a sudden had his faith restored in his son. He was doing it because he was sick of arguing about it.

Shane wanted to tell them how grateful he was, that he really wanted to be with them, that he loved them and needed them, but the words stuck in his throat. He could always form what he wanted to say in his head, but it never came out right, if it came out at all.

"What you did tonight, Shane ..." his father said suddenly. "Your mother and I think you should get counselling."

"Counselling?? Dad, I'm not crazy. I'm just ... confused."

His father just looked at him and shook

his head sadly. "All the more reason for you to get counselling, then."

Shane was silent for a moment, then he nodded. It might even be nice to have someone to talk to.

"Through the church, of course." Shane's face fell. "There's a minister from another church who'd be happy to see you once a week."

"Couldn't I just go to a regular counsellor?"

"Son, you need to get on the right track again. I really think this will help."

"But —"

"If you want to stay at Degrassi, you have to go." That was that. Shane didn't need anyone to tell him when his father was laying down the law. "And you have to keep up your marks."

"Okay."

"And one more thing." His father took a deep breath. "Aside from the necessary contact at school, we don't want you to see Spike."

Shane opened his mouth to protest, but his father gave him a look that made him shut up.

Then his mother broke in.

"We'll call Ms. Nelson and tell her we'll help with any expenses they might have between now and when the baby's born."

"There is absolutely no reason for you to stay involved in the matter, Shane. It's time for you to get on with your life."

Shane felt like laughing. If only it was that easy! Seeing Spike's growing stomach day after day at school was a constant reminder of their mistake.

His mother must have sensed what he was thinking. Suddenly she grasped his hand, surprising him. It was the first time she'd shown him any affection in a while. "Try to understand, dear." She looked into his eyes. "We truly are trying to do what's best for you. It's just that we don't really *know* what's best."

"Your mother's right Shane," his father interjected. "When we were your age, problems like this didn't happen. Or I should say, they happened, but nobody talked about them."

Shane sat silent in his chair. He felt grateful to his parents for trying to explain, but he didn't know what to say. He was finally about to speak when his mother released his hand and sat upright again.

"Do you agree with these rules?" his father asked.

Shane nodded, feeling like he was in a court of law. It wasn't like he had seen much of Spike out of school lately anyway. Besides, if he could just do all the things his parents asked, maybe he could make them proud of him again.

He looked up and caught them looking at each other, shaking their heads. He thought, "They really do think I'm crazy." Then a frightening thought occurred to him. "Maybe I am. Maybe I *am*."

CHAPTER 11

Shane waited for Spike outside school, leaning against a big oak tree. Its trunk was scarred with whittled graffiti. Shane had always thought that one day he would put his and Spike's initials on the tree — SM and SN — with a heart around them. Now it was too late.

When he saw Ms. Nelson's car drive up, he hid behind the tree. Spike got out and headed in his direction.

He stepped out from behind the tree to block her path. She hesitated, then said "Hi."

"Hi," he said, suddenly shy. "Um … sorry about the restaurant."

Spike shrugged, but then she looked closely at him. "Do you really want the baby?"

"I don't know," he sighed. "I have to get counselling."

"Well … maybe that's good." He wondered if she thought he was crazy, too.

"You know," he said, "it's not as easy being the guy as people think." Spike looked at him and smiled. She didn't really believe him, he knew, but at least she smiled and didn't give him a lecture. Then she walked away.

Shane watched her go, thinking it was strange how completely she had managed to leave him behind. Not that he blamed her. He had given her a lot of time and a lot of reasons to grow to hate his guts after she had announced she was pregnant. Now, no matter how hard he tried, he couldn't bring her back. She had made the decision that it would be easier to deal with the matter without him.

At least the baby would be born in about five months. Maybe then they could try to become normal teenagers again.

Shane looked at the school. It was the end of February. Perhaps his parents were right. Maybe it was time to get on with his life. He walked toward the building, trying to keep his head up.

CHAPTER 12

The rest of the year wasn't bad. It wasn't particularly good, but it wasn't bad, either. Shane kept reminding himself that at least it was an improvement over the long winter months.

Certain things were better than others. His relationship with his parents improved, sort of. They were cautiously kind to him, treating him like he was a mentally insane criminal who could be set off at the slightest upset. They still didn't trust him. Whenever he came home late from school, he knew the conversation that awaited him.

"Hello, Shane," his mother would say with false brightness. "How was school?"

"Fine."

There would be a pause as Shane crossed over to the fridge to get out an apple. Then his mom would turn around from whatever she was preparing on the counter and say, "It's a little bit late for you to be getting home."

"I stayed in the library. We have a history assignment due next week."

His mom would sigh and turn back to her cooking.

"I wasn't with Spike, if that's what you're thinking," he would say, knowing full well that's what she was thinking.

What bugged him most was that it was true. He never saw Spike outside of school. She didn't want to see him. And as the year drew to a close, Shane wasn't sure he wanted to be with her, either. He had taken his parents' advice and he was just trying to get on with his life. It hurt him that they couldn't see that.

They also gave him a curfew. He had to be home by ten o'clock at the latest on the weekends, and that was only if he could map out definite plans. But it didn't really matter. He didn't have anywhere to go or anyone to go out with.

At least the pressure had let up at school. Kids were finally talking to him again and, sometimes, after school, one of the guys from his gym class would ask him if he wanted to shoot some baskets or play football.

He liked the small group of guys who usually met out on the court or in the field. There were a few regulars: Snake, a tall, gangly freckle-faced boy; BLT, a good-looking, muscular black guy who was always cracking jokes; and Luke, a reserved, handsome olive-skinned guy. Shane couldn't figure Luke out. Snake and BLT were always fooling around and laughing, but Luke always looked serious. Cool, Shane thought. Luke never asked him to play basketball. It was always Snake or BLT who extended the invitation. He got the feeling Luke didn't like him very much, but who could blame him? Next to Luke, Shane felt like a gigantic wimp.

He always felt a sense of relief when Snake or BLT would ask him to join them. It meant he didn't have to go home right away, and it gave him a chance to hang around with the guys a bit. For a while, he'd felt the only human contact he had was with his parents, and that was mediocre at best.

Every Wednesday night Shane went to see Mr. Francis, the minister of another church downtown, for counselling. At first, Shane really wanted to talk. He wanted to get a lot of things off his chest. But whenever he tried to explain how he was feeling, Mr. Francis would bring it back to the same thing.

"I've just felt ... so ... alone," Shane would say. It wasn't easy, spilling his guts to a total stranger.

"You aren't alone," the minister would say. "God is with you, always."

But that was no comfort to Shane. If God was around, he couldn't feel His presence.

"At night," he would try again, "I can't sleep sometimes. Some nights, I lie awake till morning."

"You should pray in moments like that, son. Or read from your Bible. God's words are always a comfort for a troubled spirit."

But praying or reading the Bible didn't calm his troubled spirit. He felt so unsure about so many things, and his belief in God was one of them. He thought of telling Mr. Francis this, but he decided it would be easier if he just didn't rock the boat.

Even though he disliked the meetings, he kept going because he knew how much it pleased his parents. He started telling Mr. Francis how much better he felt, hoping that eventually it would be decided that he didn't have to go anymore. And one day, he got his wish.

"We've decided you don't have to see Mr. Francis after school's finished," his dad told him one night. Shane's face lit up. This surely meant that his parents' faith in him was restored and they could start working at being a normal family again.

But his smile soon faded. "We want to send you to camp," his father continued. "Bible camp. You'll be an assisant counsellor up there. It's all organized." Shane was amazed at the number of decisions that were made about him behind his back.

"But I want to be with you and Mom this summer," he blurted out, surprising himself. "Can't I get a job in Toronto?" He was also thinking of Spike. The baby would be due around August. Even though they weren't close anymore, it didn't seem right for him to be away when she had the baby.

His father studied him for a second. "Shane, I'll be honest with you. Your mother and I … we're tired. This has been an exhausting year." Shane lowered his head. He knew what his dad was getting at. "I think it would do your mother a lot of good to let her have a couple of months of peace." His dad was just confirming what Shane had felt for a long time. In his parents' eyes, he was a burden. Not a pleasure, a great kid to have around the house, a kid to make them proud. A burden.

He swallowed hard. "Okay," he said quietly.

Then he left the room, biting his bottom

lip hard. There was no way he was going to cry in front of his father again. He had tried so hard, but instead of accepting him back, they were getting rid of him.

As he went into his bedroom, his thoughts drifted back to Spike. Maybe he would be back before the baby was born. At least then he could be at the hospital to show her he cared.

And that would be that. He knew he wouldn't be able to see the baby. Their child would go off to some unknown home, and grow up never knowing about Spike or Shane, his real mom and dad. Or maybe one day, he — or would it be a she?— would come looking for them.

Shane thought about what he might say in that situation. He had no idea.

CHAPTER 13

"Love is all you need, love is all you need." The sound system in the gym pumped out the repetitious lyrics. Shane stood near the food table, dressed in a suit. Practically every student at Degrassi Junior High was there. It was the grade eight graduation.

Shane felt great. He didn't even mind the fact that the Board of Education had attached a grade nine onto Degrassi. A lot of kids were angry that they weren't going to be allowed to go to a real high school. But Shane knew what would happen if he went to another school. It would be great for about a month, because no one there would know about his past. Then, slowly at first, the rumour would spread, until it gathered speed and every single person, from grade nine to grade thirteen, knew about him and Spike.

Then the looks and the whispers would start all over again. At least at Degrassi, people had started to get bored with the subject.

Shane's exams had gone well, and he was leaving for camp the next day. During the last month of school, he had grown used to the idea of going to camp. It was over three hours away from Toronto, so at least he could be anonymous.

He saw Spike come into the gym with Heather and Erica. It was hard to believe that the baby wasn't due for another two months. She looked like she was about to burst.

When a slow song came on, he got up his nerve and walked over to her.

"Uh ... wanna dance?" he asked hesitantly.

Spike looked up from her glass of punch and threw a look at Heather and Erica. "Sure." She handed her glass to Erica. They went onto the dance floor. Shane pulled her as close as he could, but her stomach got in the way. He pretended not to notice.

But suddenly he felt something.

"Oh my God," he said, startled.

Spike smiled. "Did you feel that, too? That was the baby kicking."

Shane just stared at her. Then, without even thinking, he found his hand reaching toward her stomach.

Spike looked at him and nodded, so he placed his hand on her belly and felt the baby kick again. "Wow!"

"She's been getting pretty restless lately," Spike said.

"She?"

"Yeah. I think it's a she."

"That would be nice," Shane said softly, realizing he felt like crying for the first time in a while. He started to pull her close again, when Mr. Raditch, their English teacher/disc jockey, took off the record.

"And now, everyone, a special surprise. Degrassi's very own band, the Zit Remedy!"

Spike squeezed Shane's hand, then walked back to the front to be with her friends again.

The curtains opened, and Shane found a spot near the back to watch the antics of Joey, Wheels and Snake. He remembered a time when he had longed to be a part of their gang. He even used to dream about being in the Zit Remedy, although he couldn't play a musical instrument.

They were awful, but it didn't matter. Everyone cheered them anyway, and he let himself get wrapped up in their song.

Nothing could have prepared him for what happened next.

CHAPTER 14

Spike *did* burst. She went into labour during the Zit Remedy's song and she was rushed out of the gym.

The news spread like wildfire through the gym. As soon as it reached Shane, he tried to follow her, but she was already gone. Her mom had picked her up within minutes. Heather and Erica were still standing by the door, and they told him which hospital she had gone to.

But he never made it there. When he went outside, he saw his parents' car waiting out front. He had forgotten that they were picking him up at ten.

"Absolutely not," his father said when Shane asked if they could go to the hospital. "She'll be perfectly fine without you there. Even if you went, you wouldn't be able to see her, or the baby."

"Besides," put in his mother, "you leave for camp at seven o'clock in the morning."

It sounded ludicrous. Here he was, about to go to summer camp and become a father at the same time.

He slouched down in the back seat, suddenly overcome with exhaustion. He couldn't bring himself to argue with them the night before he was leaving. As he watched the lights of the city zoom by, he felt like Charlie Brown. Wishy-washy.

He didn't sleep all night. Every half hour he called the hospital. At first they didn't want to give him any information.

"Who's calling, please?" the nurse asked on the other end.

"I'm the father!" he squealed, his voice cracking. He was sure he sounded like a twelve year old. The nurse didn't say anything for a moment, then told him to wait.

She must have gone to ask Spike's mom, because when she came back to the phone she said she had no news yet, but he could call again. Shane could hear the reprimanding tone in her voice. She must have wondered why he wasn't there.

At six o'clock in the morning, while his mom prepared breakfast, they still had no news. At six-thirty, as his parents carried his camp gear to the car, yelling at him to hurry, he tried the hospital once more.

"Congratulations," said the nurse on the other end. "You're the father of a little baby girl."

He didn't remember getting to the bus station.

"Be good," his mom said, giving him a hug.

"And don't worry, son," his dad said, frowning as he took in Shane's dazed expression. "The baby will be put into a loving, caring home."

Shane nodded slightly. "Um ..." he started, hesitant. "Will you visit me?" Inside, he couldn't believe he was a *parent*, and was worried about missing his mom and dad.

"Of course we'll visit," his mother reassured him.

His parents waited outside the bus until it drove away. Not because they were going to miss him, Shane thought. They just wanted to make sure he actually left, that he didn't jump off the bus to go to the hospital.

Shane dozed the whole way to camp, unable to think of anything, except that Spike had been right. It was a girl.

CHAPTER 15

For the first couple of weeks, Shane hated camp. During the small amount of free time he had, he dreamed up ways to escape so he could travel back to Toronto and see Spike. He wrote her letters every night, staying in the cabin rather than joining in the parties that the other counsellors held in the dining hall after the kids had gone to bed.

One of the other counsellors, a boy Shane thought was too loud and obnoxious, tried to crack his shell a few times. His name was Chuck, and all the other guys thought he was great. But Shane avoided him, because he was sure Chuck made fun of him behind his back.

Two weeks after his arrival, he blew up. It was the first visiting day for the young campers, and Shane and the other counsel-

68

lors were on their best behaviour to greet the parents.

One of the campers' mothers had a newborn baby with her. Shane happened to be with Chuck when they welcomed her.

He couldn't keep his eyes off the tiny child.

"What a cute baby," Chuck cooed politely. "Is it a boy or a girl?"

"A girl," the mother beamed. "She's only fifteen days old."

Fifteen days old, thought Shane. That's how old Spike's baby — their baby — was. He wondered if she looked like this, fragile and adorable. He knew he was staring, but he couldn't help it.

"We're so happy," the mother said proudly. "She's our little miracle."

"She's not adopted, is she?" Shane blurted out.

The mother looked at him, confused. "No."

He felt his throat tighten. That's when he started to run. He ran as fast as he could, away from the people and toward the water. He heard Chuck yell after him, but he kept running until he was out on the dock, where he finally stopped. He sat down, panting.

The dock shook with another person's weight. Shane didn't even look up as Chuck plopped down beside him.

"Okay," he said between breaths, "what's

up? You've been walking around like your family was axe-murdered ever since you got here."

Shane was about to say "nothing" when he realized tears were streaming down his face uncontrollably. "You really want to know?" he said angrily. "Fine."

And he spilled the whole story — about Spike, his parents and the baby.

When he finished, Chuck was silent.

"There," Shane said defiantly. "Now you know, and you can tell everyone else. Maybe it's for the best. I'll get kicked out of here and I can go home."

Chuck looked at him. "I'm not telling anybody," he said quietly.

They sat in silence for a few minutes.

"You ever windsurfed?" Chuck asked suddenly.

"No," Shane replied, confused.

"I can teach you. If you want me to," Chuck added quickly.

Shane shrugged. "Sure."

Chuck broke into a grin. "And you know what? If you let yourself, you're gonna have a damn good summer." He slapped Shane on the back, still grinning broadly. Shane couldn't help himself; he smiled back.

CHAPTER 16

Chuck was right. Camp ended up being two months of calm after an exceptionally long storm. Shane was sure it was the best time of his life.

He still thought about Spike. But one night, as he thought that he might be able to get to Toronto on a weekend pass, he suddenly realized it was the last thing in the world he wanted to do.

He and Chuck became inseparable. Shane had never had such a close friend before, except for Wai-Lee, and they had been friends out of necessity, not choice.

Chuck was so easy-going and sure of himself, and everyone liked him. Shane was proud to be his best friend. And Chuck accepted him exactly as he was; he *liked* him exactly as he was. For a while Shane even wondered if it was one huge set-up, a big practical joke Chuck was planning at his expense. But he finally started to relax.

He made other friends, too. It was so easy — easier than it had ever been at Degrassi. At camp, nobody except Chuck knew about his past, and Chuck stuck faithfully to his vow of secrecy. He was just plain old Shane McKay, a normal fourteen-year-old teenager.

Being an assistant counsellor turned out to be a lot more fun than he had expected, too. It was nice having all the young kids look up to him. He was told by his seniors that he had a real knack with children. This made him smile. He wished Spike and his parents could hear them say that.

Many nights he thought about Spike and the little baby girl that might have already been adopted. He still wrote long letters to Spike, telling her about camp and asking for more information about their baby, but he never got a reply.

This bothered him, but not enough for him to do anything about it. He felt so removed from it all now, so far away. For the first time in over six months he was happy.

He was just one of the boys. At night, as he and five of the other counsellors lay in their bunks, they talked about their favourite topics: cars, partying, and girls.

One night, the conversation veered to sex.

"I almost did it," said Jeff as he tried to hit Chuck with some week-old cheese balls he had found under his sleeping bag. "With this girl, last summer. Man, we did everything but."

"What is it with girls, anyway?" whined Bill, a pimply-faced guy. "They don't mind you doing all the other stuff, but when it comes to going one little step further, that's when they suddenly get all righteous."

Greg, who had the bunk below Bill, laughed. "What do you know about it, anyway?"

Bill threw his pillow down at Greg. "Bet I know just as much as you do."

"What about you, Shane?" Jeff spoke up.

"Huh?"

"You ever done it? Had sex?"

Shane remembered a time when he was absolutely bursting to tell someone about his "sexual conquest." Now, he just moved further down into his sleeping bag and glanced over at Chuck, who was watching him. "No," he said simply. "Never."

And he didn't even feel like he was lying. Here at camp, he felt like a snake that had shed its skin. The shell of the old Shane was probably still lying somewhere in Toronto, but here at camp was a new, revitalized, improved model. The past seemed unreal.

CHAPTER 17

"Shit," said Shane as he fell off the windsurfer again. Swearing was one of the many little habits he had picked up from Chuck over the summer. At home, his parents absolutely forbade swearing, and he had obeyed them so completely that he never even swore at school like a lot of the other kids did.

But Chuck sounded so cool when he swore, and without even being conscious of it, Shane started dropping "shit" and "damn" into his own vocabulary.

He got back onto the board again and fell off almost immediately. "Damn! Damn!" he shouted, pounding the board with his fist.

"Whoa!" yelled Chuck from his board, "What's wrong with you today?" Shane stopped hitting the windsurfer and looked up. "You're being a total loser on the board today. A bigger loser than usual! *Something's* bothering you."

Shane found it easy to be open with Chuck, something he had never experienced with anyone before. They had had lots of heart-to-hearts this summer, and Chuck was a great advice giver. So Shane had no problem opening up now.

"I got a letter from my parents," he confessed.

"More parental bull?" asked Chuck.

Shane nodded. "They were supposed to visit this weekend, but now they have to go to some church conference, so they can't make it."

Chuck stared at him, incredulous. "And *that's* what you're upset about?"

Again Shane nodded, but hesitantly this time.

"Man, I'd be thrilled if my parents didn't come near this camp all summer!"

"Don't you get along with them?"

"It's not that," Chuck continued. "It's just that I'm a teenager. I'm old enough to look after myself. My parents don't think so, but I know they're wrong. I don't need them. I'm independent. And *you* should learn to be, too."

"I'm independent," Shane defended himself weakly.

"No, you're not," Chuck argued. "You're still totally dependent on your mommy and daddy, even though it sounds like they've pulled some pretty stupid moves on you."

Shane was taken aback. Nobody had ever talked about his parents that way before. "They may have been stupid moves, but they were only trying — "

" — to do what's best for you," Chuck mimicked. "Wake up! That's the oldest line in the parental handbook. They always try to make you think that the crummy things they pull are for *you*, but they're not. They're for them. They love having control. Being a parent is a power trip."

Shane stared at Chuck, amazed. His friend seemed to have a philosophy on every subject, and they all seemed to make sense. "I guess ..." he said slowly.

"My motto is, 'You can't let them push you around. You've got to look out for number one. If you've gotta count on *someone*, then count on one of your friends.'"

Shane grinned. "That's three mottoes, goofball."

Chuck splashed him with water, laughing. "Listen, the sooner you let go of the old apron strings, the better. You're practically an adult. You've got to become your *own* person, not some little clone of what your parents want you to be." He pulled a muscle-man pose. "Like me. I'm my *own* person."

"Gross. You think there's any way you could exchange the merchandise?"

Chuck glared. "Water fight!" he shouted. They splashed each other until they were both laughing uncontrollably, sputtering up water.

"Here at camp, we're freeeee!" yelled Chuck, thumping on his chest like Tarzan.

"Yeah!" shouted Shane, jumping back onto the windsurfer. "Parents! Who needs them!"

CHAPTER 18

Over the next two weeks, Shane thought a lot about what Chuck had said, and when his parents finally did visit, he decided to put his friend's advice into practice. In truth, he had missed them a lot, but he wasn't going to let *them* know that.

They sat across from him at a picnic table, at a loss for words. Shane resolved not to help them out in any way. He just sat there, playing with a piece of grass.

"What ... what kind of shirt is that?" his mom asked, trying to be pleasant.

God, he thought, didn't his mom even know what tie-dye was? It had been a huge fashion trend twenty years ago. He had learned tie-dye over the summer, and now he was teaching it to the kids in a workshop. Of the six plain white shirts his mom had sent up with him, only one remained white, and Shane was planning on dyeing it tomorrow.

"Tie-dye."

"You need anything? More socks? Underwear?" his dad asked.

Shane had the distinct impression that the picnic table wasn't really a picnic table, but a long desk in a prison, with a thick piece of bullet-proof plastic running down the middle of it, separating him from his parents.

"No."

"How are the Bible classes here?" asked his mom.

Shane looked right at them. "Boring." He knew he was being rude, but in a strange way, it felt good. In a way, Shane thought, they deserved it.

"Is it the teacher?" his dad asked, hopeful.

"No," Shane replied slowly. "It's the Bible."

His parents went pale. Suddenly Shane felt he had gone too far. "But it's nice here," he said quickly. "And I'm learning how to sail. And windsurf."

The silence remained for a moment. "Well. Be careful," was all his mom could say. His dad looked like he had a lump of meat caught in his throat, and Shane wished he could take back what he had said.

"Oh, my, look at the time," Mrs. McKay said, looking down at her watch. "We really have to be going."

Shane stood up. He wanted to ask them not to go yet. He wanted to apologize for what he had said and tell them he had missed them.

Instead, he said, "I've got to join Chuck anyway. He's teaching me how to windsurf."

"Do you need anything at all, dear?" His mom was doing the talking for both of them now. His father's face was still white as a sheet, and his lips were pursed.

"I could do with a few more plain white shirts," he said. His mom looked down at his tie-dyed shirt and just nodded.

Then they left.

He never received the white shirts.

CHAPTER 19

"Are you going to come back next summer?" Shane was shuffling his feet. Neither he nor Chuck was very good at saying goodbye.

"Definitely."

Shane broke into a smile. "Great. Me, too."

The bus arrived. A large sign said "Toronto" on the front. "I should get your address," he said quickly. Chuck lived in Timmins, Ontario, and Shane knew there was little chance that he would make it up there in the next year. But it would be fun to write. He was going to miss Chuck a lot.

Chuck wrote his address down on the back of an old Kleenex he had probably had in his pocket all summer. Shane took it delicately, between two fingers. The boys laughed.

"I've gotta be honest, I'm a lousy letter

writer. So if you never hear from me ..."
Chuck trailed off.

"No problem."

Chuck started to pick lint out of his pockets. Shane thought that for Chuck, this was just a typically sad day because it was the last day of summer. But for him, it meant so much more. It meant going back to a life he had grown to hate — a closet full of skeletons.

Worst of all, it meant returning to a lonely life. Before going to camp, he had grown used to being a loner. He had never enjoyed it, but at least he had been used to it. Now, after knowing what it was like to have a really good friend, he would have to get used to being a loner all over again. He was sure he would never find a friend like Chuck at Degrassi.

"All aboard, son," the bus driver called through the doors.

Chuck gave him a hard slap on the back. "See you next summer, Splash." Splash was the nickname Chuck had given Shane while he was teaching him how to windsurf, because Shane fell into the water so often. The name stuck for the rest of the summer. Shane loved it; finally, his very own nickname. But nobody would call him that back in Toronto.

He slapped Chuck back. "I'll write you, even if you don't write me," he said, climbing reluctantly onto the bus.

He found a seat by himself and looked out the window. He and Chuck waved to each other, then Shane watched as Chuck walked away. Long after he was out of sight, Shane kept staring out the window.

CHAPTER 20

It was dark when the bus pulled into the downtown Toronto terminal. Shane saw the Plymouth Reliant parked outside.

He tried to look on the bright side. After all, he was going into grade nine now. In five months he'd be fifteen. He felt that these two months away from home had made him much more mature and independent, thanks mainly to Chuck's lectures. He still felt bad that he didn't get along better with his parents, but not as bad as he had before he left for camp.

He decided he was tired of always trying to please them, only to have the door slam on his face time and time again. He had to start thinking of himself, too. Besides, he reasoned, the less he needed his parents, the less he could be hurt by them.

It worried him that he hadn't heard from Spike all summer. But when his parents had visited him, he had asked how she was doing and they said that as far as they knew, she was doing just fine. Maybe she was like Chuck. Maybe she just didn't like writing letters.

Shane saw his parents wave from the car. He picked up his duffle bag and, taking a deep breath, walked toward them.

"Hi!" he said as cheerfully as possible, as he got in the back seat.

"Hello, son." Shane noticed how relaxed they both looked. Younger, even. Suddenly he felt a wave of guilt. He knew they looked so healthy because he hadn't been around.

"How was the rest of camp?" his dad asked as he started up the car. They both seemed genuinely glad to see him.

"It was great. I'm really glad you sent me there," he said sincerely. "I learned a lot of stuff. Sailing, windsurfing … I'm a pretty good windsurfer now."

"That's good to hear," his mom said. "I think I'd be much too scared to get on one of those things."

"You shouldn't be! Some day, I'll take you, Mom. You're not too old." His mother laughed, and Shane smiled. He felt surprisingly good.

"We had a fairly quiet summer ourselves," said his dad as he drove. "Carl was home for a couple of weeks. He sends his love."

Shane felt a pang of jealousy shoot through his stomach. "That's nice."

"I forgot to mention," his mother said. "At the beginning of the summer three of your friends came over."

"What friends?"

"That tall freckle-faced boy with the funny nickname."

"Snake."

"That's it. And a big Negro boy — "

"Black!" he said, exasperated. Then, softening his tone, "Black, Mom. Nobody says Negro any more."

"Oh," she said, slightly hurt. "I certainly didn't mean anything bad by it. And the third was dark-skinned, probably from a mixed marriage — "

Shane grit his teeth. "Luke."

"Anyway, they wanted you to play basketball with them. I thought it was nice they dropped by." So did Shane. That was a good sign.

"I made a lot of friends at camp," he told them.

"That's nice," his dad said, sincere.

"And the senior counsellors want me to go back next year. They said I worked really well with the kids." He thought he saw his parents shoot a look at each other, but decided he was mistaken.

"Speaking of kids," he said slowly, "what happened? To the baby?"

They pulled into their driveway. There was silence as his father turned off the ignition.

Shane didn't like the silence. It meant something bad.

"Did she ... die?" he said in a whisper.

"No," his dad said. "Shane, we didn't tell you this when we saw you in July because we didn't want you to worry. We just wanted you to relax and enjoy yourself."

"Tell me what?" He could feel his whole body tense.

"Spike made what we feel was the wrong decision," said his mom.

"She decided to keep the baby."

Shane could hardly breathe. It had to be something about him and Toronto. He had only been back five minutes and already he felt sick.

He stared at his parents in disbelief. "You lied to me?"

"We didn't lie," his father started. "We just didn't tell you."

"Right!" Shane was yelling now. "So if I never told you about getting Spike pregnant, and sooner or later you found out from some-one else, I could say I didn't lie, I just didn't tell you."

"Calm down," his mom said.

"That was a shitty thing to do," said Shane. His parents froze.

"Don't you ever let me hear you say that word again, young man," Mr. McKay said.

Shane flung open the back door and hopped out with his duffle bag. He stood in the driveway and yelled as loudly as he could.

"Shit! Shit! Shit!" He slammed the back door of the car.

CHAPTER 21

Shane was a bundle of nerves as he headed up the front steps of Degrassi. But the other kids were actually saying hi to him, which put him slightly more at ease.

He was wearing one of his new tie-dye creations. When he had come down for breakfast that morning his mother had looked at his shirt, startled.

"Oh Shane! You're not going to wear that to school, are you?"

"Yeah," he'd said stubbornly. "Why shouldn't I?"

"But what about all those new shirts I bought you?"

"Mom," he had said impatiently, "I think I'm old enough to choose my own clothes. Besides, those shirts you bought are gross." With that, he had grabbed his books, his lunch and an apple and started to leave the kitchen, ignoring the hurt look on his mother's face.

"What about breakfast?"

"I'm already late," was his brief answer as he had rushed out the front door and slammed it behind him.

He was still angry with them. That made it a lot easier to put Chuck's theories into practice. But one of his theories had been, "If you have to count on someone, count on one of your friends." Shane needed someone to count on. But he didn't have any friends.

Now he went into the office to get his new locker number. Doris Bell, the school secretary, stood at the counter, issuing all the essentials for the first day of school: floor plans for new students, floor plans for a few disoriented returning students, locks and locker numbers.

When she saw him, she smiled. "Hello, there," she said in her jolly voice. "Welcome back to Degrassi, Shane."

"Thanks, Doris," he said sincerely.

"Hey, Shane," said a disinterested voice behind him.

He turned around and saw Luke, who looked even cooler this year, decked out in a Gourmet Scum T-shirt, torn jeans and black sneakers.

"Hi, Luke," he said, suddenly feeling shy. "How's it goin'?"

"Great, really ... uh ... great. And you?"

"Okay," said Luke, without a smile. He looked bored. Boy, he was cool as a cucumber, Shane thought.

"Okay, considering it's the first day back at school?" Shane tried to joke.

"I hate it here."

As they left the office together, Shane eyed Luke admiringly. To be half as cool as that!

Luke headed in the opposite direction. "See ya," was all he said.

"Uh ... maybe we can shoot some baskets after school," Shane called after him, hoping he didn't sound overly enthusiastic.

"Maybe."

Shane watched him go. In some ways, Luke reminded him of Chuck. He realized with a pang that he already missed Chuck, and only twenty-four hours had passed since he had last seen him.

"Oh, well," he sighed as he continued down the hall and started up the stairs to his locker. "You'd better get used to your *own* charming company."

Suddenly his walk slowed to a crawl. He heard girls' voices on the stairs up ahead.

"How was the delivery?" He recognized the voice of Alexa, the bubbliest girl at Degrassi.

91

Then he heard an even more familiar voice. "Really painful. I was in labour for almost ten hours."

He felt his heart tighten.

When his parents had told him Spike had decided to keep the baby, Shane knew it was true, but he had tried to push it from his mind. He couldn't help but think she had made a mistake, too. How could either of them get on with their lives now?

And now, standing here and listening to the conversation on the stairs above him, there was no point denying the truth.

He had an overwhelming urge to run back down the stairs and out of the school, back home, where he could beg his parents to send him to private school immediately.

"Emma. That's such a pretty name," said Heather.

Emma. Shane whispered the name slowly to himself. "Emma." It sounded so ... dainty.

"I named her after my grandma," Spike explained.

"How long was she in the hospital?" asked Alexa.

"Six weeks." Six weeks! thought Shane as he continued to eavesdrop. "She was hooked up to a heart monitor and everything. She almost died. She still has to go in twice a week for checkups. It's exhausting."

Shane felt tears forming in his eyes, and he could feel a big lump crawling into his throat.

"Taking care of a baby's tough. I didn't go to one party all summer." Shane knew that for Spike, this was highly unusual.

"So who's taking care of Emma now?" asked Liz.

"This girl I met in prenatal classes — she's a waitress. She takes care of Emma when I'm in school, and I take care of her baby in the evenings. That's why I can never go out anywhere."

"Can't you get a babysitter?"

"How? I don't have any money."

Shane took a deep breath, clenched his fists, and continued up the stairs.

CHAPTER 22

"She's so small," Alexa said, studying a photograph.

"Well, she was premature," said Spike. She froze when Shane's hand intervened and took the picture.

Shane stared at Spike, then at the photo. "Is that Emma?" he said in a whisper.

Silence descended upon the group. Shane felt like he was in one of those bad horror movies, where all the nice, normal people suddenly turn into killer zombies.

Finally, Spike spoke. "How nice you're interested, after hiding all summer."

Shane looked at her, flabbergasted. "I wasn't hiding! I told you months ago my parents were sending me to camp."

He was sure they had been talking about him earlier. Nothing else could explain the cold looks he was getting from Spike and her friends.

She tried to grab the picture away from him, but he held on to it stubbornly. Perhaps she didn't want the picture to rip, because she eased her grip and finally let go.

"Didn't you read my letters?" he asked her.

"I didn't open them," she replied smugly.

This was all too weird. She *knew* he was going to camp. It was *her* choice to keep the baby. What did she expect from him?

"Please, Spike," he said slowly. "I want to help. She's my responsibility, too."

"Yeah? You want to come over and change her diaper some time?" she sneered as she stood up. It was strange to see her slim again. She and her friend Liz started to walk away.

"Couldn't you let me see her? Please?" he called after her.

"Somehow I don't think that would thrill your parents," she shot back as she disappeared through the doors.

The other kids still stood there, looking at their shoes. Slowly, they wandered away, leaving Shane alone on the stairway, wondering what Spike had been talking about.

But the bell rang, interrupting his train of thought. He started to run up the stairs, not

95

wanting to be late on his first day back. Quickly he found his locker and started to put his things away. Then he noticed that he still held something in his hand. The photo of Emma. She was still in her incubator in the picture. A tuft of black hair stuck out from her head. She looked more like a little monkey than a baby.

He cradled the picture. Emma. She looked so shrivelled and fragile. So beautiful.

He stuck the picture up on the inside of his locker, then hurried to class, determined to have a long talk with Spike before the day was over.

CHAPTER 23

He didn't get a chance to talk to Spike until the end of the day. But all afternoon, he thought about the things he had heard her say, and he had come up with some ideas of his own.

He felt proud of himself. His ideas weren't outrageous this time. He didn't want to marry her. He didn't want custody. He didn't want to create a scene like he had months ago in that restaurant. He just wanted to help. It would be the first step in proving his new independence.

He was at his locker, staring at the picture of Emma, when Luke came up behind him.

"Still want to shoot some baskets?"

"Great! Sure," Shane said, taken aback. Luke looked over his shoulder at the picture.

"That your kid?"

"Yeah." It felt funny saying that. Yeah. *His* baby.

"Wow. Sure doesn't look like you. Not yet, anyway."

BLT joined them. "You coming?" Luke and BLT started to walk away.

"Um ... I'll be out in a few minutes." Shane glanced over to where Spike stood, talking to Liz.

"Sure, no sweat," said Luke. Shane liked his easy-going attitude. Like Chuck, Luke wasn't the type to bother gossiping about anyone. He minded his own business, and probably expected the same from others.

Shane walked toward Spike.

"Spike?" he said hesitantly, interrupting her conversation with Liz.

"I asked you to leave me alone," she said coolly.

"Fine. But ..." He dug into his pocket and came up with a crumpled five dollar bill. He handed it to her. "Here."

"What's this?"

"Half my allowance. I'd give you more, but I need the rest for bus fare and stuff." She was just looking at him. "It's sort of like child support."

They stood in silence as Spike quietly put the five dollars into her pocket. "Couldn't we please just talk for a few minutes? Alone?"

he pleaded.

She softened. "Sure. I'll meet you outside, Liz," she said to her friend. They walked downstairs to a little alcove in the basement. The only person who ever came down there was the janitor, and she would be busy cleaning the classrooms.

"I'm also going to get a part-time job after school so I can give you more," Shane announced proudly.

"I — thanks."

"I just figured, I'm old enough. And it's what lots of divorced people do. And we're kind of divorced." His voice cracked on the last word. To his surprise, Spike leaned over and took his hand.

"I guess I shouldn't have been so mean," she said. "But I really hoped you'd at least visit when you found out I decided to keep her."

"But I only found out yesterday."

Spike's eyes widened. "You mean your parents didn't tell you? I asked them to get in touch with you!" She shook her head. "Your parents can be total jerks."

"Yeah," he said bitterly. "Believe it or not, they thought they were doing what was best for me."

Spike studied him for a moment. "You know, you look different this year. Not quite so … uptight."

He laughed in spite of himself. "I think camp did it to me."

They were silent for a moment. "I'm really sorry I wasn't around when you had the baby. I called the hospital every half hour."

"Really? Nobody told me."

"I guess *your* mom thought she was doing what was best for you."

She smiled. "Parents! Oh, no … I guess I can't say that anymore. I *am* a parent. I think I'm beginning to see just how tough it is."

"But still," he asserted, "I'll *never* screw up as much as my parents."

"I wouldn't be so hard on them," she replied. "We've kind of screwed up a lot ourselves."

Shane was silent.

"But really," she continued, "it's tough. Like, with Emma, I always want to do the right thing, feed her at the right time, check on her during the night, dress her warmly enough, hold her when she cries … and even *that's* exhausting and easy to screw up."

"Imagine when she's a teenager!" Shane joked, and they both laughed.

Then he got serious again. "Can I see her? Emma?"

Spike hesitated. "I don't know. She's still pretty sick."

"I won't even pick her up. I'll just look at her."

She sighed. "All right. Not yet, though. Soon. But what about your parents? I know they don't want you hanging around me, or the baby."

"I just won't tell them," he said without thinking. It would be so much easier to lie to them than to tell them the truth. Lying was clean and simple. Telling the truth always ended up in a huge argument, with Shane never getting his way and all of them feeling miserable.

"Besides, my parents did the same thing by not telling me about you, right?"

"I guess," she shrugged, glancing at her watch. "I've gotta go. My babysitting shift starts soon."

"Spike?" She stopped and looked at him. "Why'd you do it? What made you keep the baby?"

She lowered her head. "If you could've seen her ... she was so helpless. And she was crying and crying .... Then they let me hold her for a minute. And she stopped crying. Just holding her ... there was no way I could give her up. I felt she needed me so bad ...."

He understood what she meant. He would love to be needed like that.

They walked out of school together.

CHAPTER 24

Shane's parents were surprised when he announced that he wanted to get a part-time job.

"Isn't your allowance enough?" his mother wanted to know.

"It's not the money, really. I, uh ... just feel I can take on the extra responsibility."

"What about your marks?" his dad asked.

"I can keep them up. I just want to work once or twice a week."

"Where are you going to find this job?"

He hesitated. "I don't know, yet. But tons of places hire students part-time."

"I don't know," said Mrs. McKay. "You're only fourteen, after all."

"*Only* fourteen?? Anyway, I'm fifteen in five months. Lots of kids my age have jobs."

His parents frowned, but Shane was

prepared. He had lots of ammunition.

"Think of all the money I can save for university. Money that won't have to come out of your savings."

"True," his dad said with a little more interest. "But still ..."

"Look," Shane continued. "There's no harm in letting me try. If it doesn't work out, I'll just quit."

They looked at each other. Then his dad spoke. He always got the final word. "Okay. But on a few conditions. We approve of the job. You keep your marks up. And you stay away from Spike and the baby."

Shane felt his anger rise quickly to the surface. These days it seemed to be bubbling away just below his skin, ready to boil over at any moment when he was around his parents.

"Please, dear," his mother cut in. "I know we don't always make the best decisions. But we're sticking by this one."

"You *must* get on with your own life, son," his dad said, almost pleading. "Staying involved with her will only drag you down."

"That's right. She's made her bed. She's the one who must lie in it."

"Sure," Shane mumbled as he quickly left the room. As he walked upstairs, he thought that his mother had made a poor choice of clichés.

CHAPTER 25

It wasn't as easy getting a job as Shane thought it would be. He had absolutely no experience, and even McDonald's didn't seem to be hiring.

He decided to ask BLT and Luke if they had any suggestions, when they stopped to take a short rest from their basketball game one afternoon.

They had been playing regularly since the beginning of school, but despite the fact that someone always asked him to join them, Shane still didn't feel like part of the gang. When the games were over, nobody invited him for fries, or to the video parlour. He would walk home alone, hoping that there would be a letter from Chuck waiting for him; but there never was, even though he had written Chuck twice already.

He felt the most lonely on the weekends. When the phone rang, he would race to answer it, hoping it was someone from school inviting him somewhere; but it never was.

Luke still intrigued him. Even though they had played basketball together almost every school day for a couple of weeks, Shane still couldn't figure him out. He was really distant, and Shane wasn't sure if Luke liked him or not. But he admired the way Luke never revealed his emotions. He wished he could be more like him. Shane felt like everyone could always see what he was feeling, and he hated it.

And he wasn't the only one who admired Luke. A lot of the girls liked him, too. But Luke just took it with a grain of salt. Sometimes he had a girlfriend, sometimes he didn't. He said he got bored with them easily. Shane only wished he had that problem! Girls still avoided him like the plague, as if going out on one date with him would give them an instant bad reputation.

Today, when BLT called "Time," Shane got up the nerve to ask their advice.

"Either of you guys know where I could get a job?"

BLT shook his head. "My parents won't let me work till I'm fifteen."

"Man, you've got to show your parents

who's boss," Luke snorted.

Shane thought he sounded just like Chuck. "I want to give some money to Spike, for the baby."

"Man, if it was me, I'd forget about her. It was her decision to keep the kid," said Luke.

Shane shook his head. "It's not that easy."

Luke thought for a moment. "I can get you a job, I bet."

Shane tried not to show too much excitement. "Really? That would be great. Where?"

"I work at this burger joint near my place. The owner's been looking for extra help."

It sounded too good to be true. Imagine a job at the same place as Luke! And the fact that Luke was suggesting it must mean he thought Shane was okay.

"We can go tomorrow after school," said Luke.

"All right!"

Shane grabbed the basketball from BLT and tossed it through the air toward the basket. It slipped through the hoop, a perfect shot.

CHAPTER 26

"Okay, kid, you've got the job." Shane was standing behind the counter with Luke, looking at the big fat man who owned the restaurant. His name was Joe, and his burger joint was called Joe's Burger Joint.

Shane thought it was perfect, even though he knew the place was what his parents would call a greasy spoon, and it wasn't exactly located in the best part of downtown.

Joe wiped his hands on the front of his grease-stained apron. "Pay's not great. I don't make a fortune here, you know." Shane waited. "Four dollars an hour. Four twenty-five after three months."

Four dollars an hour! It sounded like a small fortune. At that rate, he would only have to work five hours to raise the twenty dollars a week he wanted to give Spike. After that, the rest would be his to spend on whatever he pleased.

"How many shifts do you think I'll get?"

"I'll start you off with two. Every Tuesday after school, from four to nine. And every Saturday, from eleven to ten, with a paid hour for lunch. That's my busiest day."

Shane quickly calculated it in his head. That meant sixteen hours a week. Sixty-four dollars a week! He could buy all kinds of new clothes, and maybe even save up for his own stereo....

"Since you two are friends, I'll put Luke on the same shifts as you, at least for a while. You'll be his trainer, Luke."

Luke smiled. Shane could tell that he and Joe liked each other, and that Joe trusted Luke. Watching them, Shane could hardly believe Luke was only a few months older than he was. He seemed so mature, even able to talk to a guy like Joe, who must be his parents' age, on an equal level.

A customer came through the door. "Hey, Joe. Gimme a cheeseburger with fries and gravy on the side."

"I've gotta get back to work," Joe said to them. "See you Tuesday, kid."

As the boys left the restaurant, Shane was beaming. "Thanks, Luke. Thanks a lot. This is fabulous."

"No problem," replied Luke nonchalantly. "Who knows? Maybe it'll be fun."

Shane hoped he was right. Certainly things were looking up. He would be making more money than he knew what to do with, he would be helping Spike, and he would be working with Luke.

Maybe they would even become friends.

CHAPTER 27

"That's it??" his mother said, staring out the car window at the blinking neon sign that said "Joe's Bu ger Jo nt." The "r" and the "i" were burned out.

"Isn't it great?" Shane couldn't help himself. He really did think it was great. His very first job.

"Oh, Lord," his father sighed. "Son, maybe I could find you some part-time work doing maintenance at the church."

Shane crossed his arms over his chest. "No way," he said. "I want to work here." He was determined to get his way this time, even if it meant arguing until he was blue in the face. He wanted this job more than he could remember wanting anything else, because it would finally give him the independence he'd been craving ever since he'd returned from camp. It had been easy to tell himself he was his own person, but he still didn't feel like he knew who his own person was. He was counting on this job to help him figure it out.

"Come on," he pleaded. "You know how long I was looking for work. Finally I find a job and you want me to quit before I've even started."

Shane knew that his father didn't like quitters. "And there's the subway, right over there," he pointed.

There was silence for a long time in the car, except for the steady purr of the engine.

"Of course," his father said suddenly. "You're right." Shane raised his eyebrows. His father was telling him he was right??

Mr. McKay turned to his wife. "I think we should let him take the job." His mom just shook her head, but Shane knew the job was his. "You know, son, when I was your age, I'd been working part-time for over a year. And it wasn't in the nicest of places, either," he chuckled.

"Where?"

"Well," continued his dad, "it was at a pub."

"Steven! Why, I never knew that."

"I was only thirteen when I started working there. Our family was barely scraping by, and I was the oldest child. Friends of my parents ran the local pub, and they gave me a job clearing tables and washing beer glasses."

"Wow," exclaimed Shane. "Tell me more." He tried to imagine his father as a teenager. He soon gave up and listened instead.

His father started to drive toward home. "It was a couple of years after the war. Most people were prospering at that time, but not us. My father was a travelling Bible salesman ..."

Shane settled back in his seat. For the first time in his entire life, his dad was talking to him like a friend instead of a father. He smiled, savouring every word his dad said. This was the kind of moment he had often dreamed of — a moment of friendship with his parents.

CHAPTER 28

But those moments were few and far between, and the very next morning Shane was arguing with his parents again.

"I've got to run. I've got to be at school early," he said as he raced through the kitchen.

"You *must* eat a balanced breakfast!" his mother insisted.

"I'm going to grab a doughnut in the cafeteria."

"Sit down, young man," his dad said sternly. "Your eggs are already cooking."

"You guys can split them. Here, I'll take a nutritious apple." He grabbed one from a bowl on the counter and started to leave.

"That is hardly a decent breakfast!" his mom shouted after him.

"Mom, come on," said Shane, feeling on top of the world in spite of himself. "I can look after myself." And with that, he was out the door.

He practically skipped to school. "I'm a working man!" he sang aloud as he hurried down the street, startling a few old ladies at a bus stop.

He waited outside the front doors of Degrassi for Spike. When she arrived, he told her. "I got a job."

"That's great! Where?"

"At Joe's Burger Joint," he said proudly. "Luke got it for me."

Spike's forehead wrinkled. "Luke?"

"Yeah. He works there, too. Isn't that great?"

"I don't know, Shane. I've heard lots of rumours."

"Like what?"

"Like that Luke does drugs and stuff."

Shane stared at her. "Spike. You of all people should *not* listen to rumours."

"True."

"Anyway, Luke's a great guy. One of the few people who's ever nice to me around here," he said with a glance toward Degrassi.

"Sorry," smiled Spike. "Just be careful."

"You sound like my parents." He rolled his eyes. "Doesn't anyone believe I can look after myself? I've got a job, don't I?"

"That's right. Congratulations." She shook his hand ceremoniously.

"But there's one condition."

Spike looked blankly at him. He had given it a lot of thought the night before, and he thought it was only fair.

"I get to see Emma." It had been almost three weeks since Spike had told him he could visit her some day after school, but every time he asked, she had some excuse.

She did now, too. "It's just that she's still pretty sick ..." she started.

But Shane didn't let her finish. "You keep saying that. And I'm sorry she's sick. But I'm not going to pass on any deadly disease to her." He slowed down. "Come on. I just want to *look* at her."

She still didn't answer.

"I won't give you any money till I see her," he finally said. "It's not fair. If I give you twenty dollars a week, I should be able to see her."

Spike lowered her head for a moment, then looked back up at him.

"Okay," she sighed. "You can come over tonight after school. My mom won't be home yet."

She walked away, while Shane stood in the middle of the steps, getting bumped by other students who were hurrying to school. But he hardly felt them. Finally, he was going to see his daughter.

CHAPTER 29

Shane stared down into the crib. "She's beautiful," he whispered, not wanting to wake her.

And he meant it. Emma had lost her shrivelled, fragile appearance. Now she looked like a bouncy, healthy baby. "She could be in baby food ads," he told Spike sincerely.

Spike laughed. "Maybe I should see about getting her an audition. The money must be great."

Suddenly, Emma's eyes opened. Shane was startled. He expected her to start crying. Instead she opened her little mouth and twisted it into a yawn. Then she belched.

"Wow! That's some loud noise for such a little thing," he laughed.

Emma looked up at Spike now, and

116

started moving around in her crib, stretching out her tiny arms.

"She wants you to pick her up," he said.

"Why don't you pick her up?"

"You mean it?"

"Just be really careful. Support her head and her back."

Shane slowly reached into the crib. He realized his hands were shaking. Carefully, he slipped one hand behind Emma's head and one hand behind her back. Then, ever so slowly, he gently lifted her out of the crib.

Spike giggled. "You're holding her like she's a smelly fish or something. You can hold her closer."

Gradually, he pulled the baby toward him. He was afraid she would start to wail at any moment, but she remained quiet. He cradled her against his chest.

Emma didn't cry. She just gurgled happily into his shoulder.

Shane held her a bit more tightly. She felt wonderful, warm and soft. He held her in front of him. "Hi, Emma! Hi! It's your daddy," he said to her, grinning like a fool. Emma grinned. "She knows who I am, Spike. I'm sure of it."

Spike just smiled. Suddenly, Emma belched again and spat up on his shirt.

Spike took her out of his arms. "Emma!"

she exclaimed. "I don't know why she'd do that. She hasn't even had her supper yet."

"It's okay," said Shane. He just kept staring at Emma while Spike held her in her arms, singing softly to her.

Shane thought he understood what a miracle was now. Emma was a miracle. For the first time in almost a year, he thought that there might very well be a God.

Before he left Spike's house, he got a cloth and cleaned off his shirt. He felt sad that he couldn't tell his parents he had been to visit Emma, but he knew it wasn't worth the trouble it would cause.

He thought back to around this time last year, when he had started telling his first lies to his parents. He remembered how his face would turn red as a beet, and he would feel guilty for days.

Now his face didn't turn red anymore, but Shane had to admit he still felt guilty. But not as much. And not as often.

He gave Emma one final kiss and left for home.

CHAPTER 30

"Toasted western with fries!" shouted Luke from the cash register to Shane, who stood sweating over the grill. Shane immediately dumped a handful of chopped ham and onions into a bowl. Then he cracked two eggs and stirred the mixture furiously. He poured the whole mess onto the hot grill and it started to sizzle.

He came home smelling like grease every time he worked. He and Luke always had the same shifts, and he noticed that Luke always took the easy jobs, like cash, while Shane worked over the grill and cleaned up in the evenings. But he didn't mind. He loved working at Joe's. And, after all, Luke *was* his supervisor. He would probably take the easy jobs, too, if he was in Luke's shoes.

He had been getting more shifts recently.

Often, he worked on Sunday, which meant he missed church. This didn't bother him, but he knew it bothered his parents. Whenever he had to work on a Sunday, he would get up early and prepare a huge, greasy breakfast for them, making the things he had learned to make at work.

"Can't you just refuse to work on Sundays?" his mom would say as she sipped on her coffee. "You know how much it means to your father to have you in church."

Shane did know, and sometimes he felt bad. But hanging around Luke *and* making money on Sunday, the day Shane usually found incredibly boring, was far more enjoyable than going to church. "Joe really needed someone," he would say as he stood over the stove frying bacon. "I couldn't say no."

"Well, it's good to see you're enjoying your job, anyway."

Shane would drop an egg into the frying pan. "Eggs over easy, or sunny side up?"

Things at home weren't nearly as tense lately, and Shane was sure it had a lot to do with his job. For one thing, it got him out of the house more often. But more important, his parents were pleased to see how seriously he took his job. He didn't even ask for his allowance anymore, and it gave him a sense of satisfaction, being "financially independent." His dad was proud of this fact, too, and he took Shane to the bank when he got his first pay cheque, to open his own account. He even matched the amount of his first deposit, giving him close to one hundred dollars in the bank.

For a while Shane did quite well saving his money, even though he always gave Spike twenty dollars a week.

Then he discovered more fun things to do with his money.

He was cleaning the restaurant one Saturday night while Luke counted the money in the register. They had been working together for a few weeks now, and even though they got along fine, their friendship still hadn't branched out beyond school and the restaurant, as Shane had hoped it would.

He knew Luke had a lot of friends in high school, because they often dropped by Joe's. If Joe wasn't around, Luke would give them free fries and chat with them while Shane stayed behind the counter, working. He envied Luke's older friends. No wonder Luke didn't want to hang around with him after work. He already had plenty of cool buddies.

So on weekends, when they closed the restaurant, Shane and Luke would part ways: Shane, to his house, where he would watch TV and go to bed; Luke, to some wild party or another. Shane knew this because Luke would almost always jokingly complain about his hangover or lack of sleep the next day. Shane, healthy and well-rested, wished he could say the same things.

He longed to "feel like crap," one of Luke's expressions. Because even if Luke didn't feel so great on Sunday, he was obviously enjoying himself far more than Shane was on Saturday night.

But this Saturday, Luke surprised him. "There's nothing going on tonight," he said despondently. "I've called everyone I know."

"Too bad," mumbled Shane as he scrubbed the grill.

Luke was quiet for a moment, then he said, nonchalantly, "Wanna come over to my place when we're done here?"

Shane looked up, surprised. "Uh ... " he answered, pretending that he was trying to remember if he had other plans. "Sure, I guess so."

"We can get some beer."

"Beer?" Shane said with a note of surprise, which he instantly regretted.

"Sure. Don't you ever drink?"

"Well, uh ... no, not really. My parents don't drink at all, so there's never anything around the house."

"Man, your parents sound boring."

"Well, yeah. I guess they kind of are."

"So. You want to come, or not?"

"Sure."

"You got money?" Luke asked. "I'm short till our next pay cheque."

"I have ten dollars," Shane said, searching his pockets. "But how are we going to get beer?"

"I've got fake I.D."

Luke handed him a plastic-coated card. It sure did look fake. Shane couldn't believe it would work.

But it did. Later that evening, Luke came walking out of the beer store with a six pack.

"Your parents know you drink?" Shane asked as they walked to Luke's.

"Sure."

Shane's mouth dropped open. "And they don't mind?"

"Sort of. But they drink, too." Luke started to laugh. "Once, my dad found a six pack in my room, right? When I got home, he started lecturing me on the evils of drinking. And you know what he was holding in his hand?" He paused dramatically. "One of *my* beers, open and half-empty already."

Shane forced a laugh, bewildered. "Ha-ha. What happened after that?"

"I called him a hypocritical bastard."

"You called your dad a bastard??"

"He's called me worse, believe me. Then I said, 'You better buy me another six pack.'"

"And did he?"

"No. But I just stole a two-four from him later."

"Uh ... what's a two-four?"

Luke studied him to see if he was kidding. "Twenty-four beers, dummy."

"Oh. Oh, yeah."

"Here we are," Luke announced.

CHAPTER 31

"This is totally amazing!" Shane exclaimed as he looked around Luke's room. It was in the basement of his parents' house, and it was full of old, wobbly pieces of furniture. A plaid pull-out couch was placed at one end of the room, and an old La-z-Boy chair sat beside it. At the other end of the room was an old black-and-white TV set, and a brand new stereo. Posters of rock bands adorned the walls, and the floor was covered with thick green shag carpeting. The room even had its own entrance through the garage.

How could one person be so lucky? Luke had everything going for him!

"Yeah. It's almost like having my own place. I hardly ever see my parents."

"Doesn't that bug them?" Shane asked.

"No. It suits us all fine. I stay out of their

way; they stay out of mine."

"Good system."

Luke opened a beer and passed it to Shane. "Thanks for the loan," he said. "I'll pay you back next week."

"No problem," replied Shane, still holding the beer. He hesitated, then took a long swig. It took a great effort on his part not to spit it back up. *This* was what beer tasted like? It was so bitter.

He took another big mouthful. By the fourth or fifth mouthful, it didn't taste so bad.

"I would love to have a place like this," Shane marvelled as he eased himself into the La-z-Boy.

"Yeah. I can come home whenever I want, leave whenever I want ... I mean, I *am* fifteen."

Shane realized that he would be fifteen, too, in less than four months, but he didn't have anywhere near the freedom Luke had. Only an hour ago he had had to beg his parents just to be allowed to come over here. Finally, he asked if he could sleep over, and they had agreed, as long as he was home in plenty of time for church the next day, since he wasn't working.

He shook his beer and realized it was already finished. Luke passed him another one, then opened a drawer and took out something wrapped in tin foil. Shane watched, curious, as he opened it. It looked like a small piece of chocolate. Luke took a match and held it to the brown stuff for a second, then crumbled some off onto a cigarette paper. Shane suddenly realized it must be hash.

"Go ahead and put on an album," said Luke. Shane went over to the record collection. There had to be a hundred albums. He flipped through them, not sure what to put on. He hadn't heard of half the bands, and he didn't want to put on anything that wasn't cool. There were a lot of Stones albums, so he figured that was a safe bet.

He started the record player. "I'm saving up to get my own stereo," he said.

The music started. "Crank it," said Luke. Shane turned up the volume so loud that he and Luke had to yell at each other, but Luke seemed to like it that way. He lit the joint and took a few long drags. Then he passed it to Shane.

Shane hesitated. "You ever smoked before?" asked Luke.

"No." He knew Luke wouldn't believe him anyway if he lied. "Just cigarettes."

Luke shrugged. "There's nothing to it. Just take a big drag and try to hold it in, like in your stomach, though, not just in your mouth, for as long as you can."

Shane held the joint between two fingers and stared at it. He'd only heard about drugs from his parents, and from films at school. The impression they all gave was that smoking one joint would probably kill him. "What ... what does it do exactly?" he asked Luke.

"Doesn't hurt you," Luke said, sounding slightly exasperated for the first time. "It just relaxes you."

Shane didn't want to do anything to ruin this evening. He had dreamed of being friends with Luke for a long time, and the last thing he needed was to have Luke think he was a wimp.

So he took a long drag. He tried to hold it in, but ended up coughing and hacking for what felt like ages. He tried again, and this time he managed to hold it in for a few seconds.

"No problem," he thought happily. "I can handle it."

Shane felt great. He sat on a cushion on the floor, laughing at everything Luke said.

"It must be a drag, knowing you've got a kid already," said Luke.

Shane started to giggle uncontrollably. "Who'd have thought it would be me? I mean, really. If you were to look around Degrassi a year ago and pick out one person who'd be a *father* by the next year, would you pick me?"

Even Luke had to laugh at that. "Well, to be honest, no." He passed Shane the mickey of rye again. They had finished the beer about an hour earlier, so Luke had snuck upstairs to his parents' liquor supply and come back down with a half bottle of rye. "Have another swig."

This was the life, Shane thought happily. He took another drink of rye.

"I can't believe you give her twenty bucks a week, man."

Shane didn't laugh much this time. "Well. You know. It is my kid, too."

"But *she's* the one who wanted to keep it. Like, what are you gonna do in a few years? She'll probably be married to someone else, or living in another city. You'll probably never see your kid again. And the only memory you'll have is that you gave her hundreds and hundreds, maybe even thousands of dollars, that you could have used to have fun."

Shane didn't have an answer for that. He had never thought that far into the future. "Hey, pass me the rye again."

He had another swig, then another, and passed the bottle back to Luke.

Suddenly he didn't feel great anymore. It happened in seconds. A wave of nausea came over him. It must have shown, because Luke asked if he was okay. Shane started to shake his head, but he didn't even have time to get up. He barfed all over the old shag carpet in Luke's bedroom.

CHAPTER 32

Shane didn't blame Luke for keeping his distance the following week. After all, it was Luke who had had to clean everything up, since Shane had passed out immediately afterward. He was completely humiliated. Just as he and Luke were finally becoming friends, he had to go and throw up on his floor. And if only it had been just a floor, not that awful, deep shag carpeting.

Luke didn't talk much to him on their Tuesday shift, except to say, "Burger and fries, hold the pickle," or "One clubhouse special." Shane just kept his mouth shut and worked.

On Friday he came into the restaurant with his head lowered. He went about his work in a daze, and twice he burned some burgers because he was staring off into space.

"Okay," Luke said after the second burger was ruined. "What's up?"

"Our mid-term report cards were given out today."

"Yeah. So?"

"My marks have dropped. Kind of a lot."

"Let's see."

Shane took out his report card and handed it to Luke. "You've got a couple of B's and a couple of C's," Luke said. "What's wrong with that?"

"It's just that I usually get A's and an occasional B." It was strange to feel embarrassed about something that used to make him so proud.

"Gee, tough."

"*I* don't really care," Shane lied. "It's my parents. They told me I could have this job *if* I kept my marks up. If they dropped, they said I had to quit."

"Man, you shouldn't let your parents get away with crap like that! You're practically an adult."

Shane shuffled his feet. "Yeah. Well."

Luke thought for a moment. "I know. Come here."

He took Shane through the back into Joe's office. There was an old typewriter sitting on the desk. "I've done this occasionally when my marks have been too bad for even *my* parents to see them," he confided, sitting down at Joe's desk. "You take some white-out, and you put a very thin layer on the letters you want to change. Then you let it dry thoroughly, like let it sit there for ten minutes. Then you line it up in the typewriter and type in your new improved grade. Your parents see it, and they sign it. No problem."

"But what about the school? Won't they check it with their records?"

"I've done it three times and never got caught. They just glance at the signature and put it in their files. Besides," he winked at Shane, "they'd never think *you* would do anything naughty like this."

Shane smiled weakly.

"Hey, listen, you don't have to do it," said Luke, starting to put the white-out back in the drawer. "It was just a suggestion."

Shane stared at his report card. If he didn't do it, Luke would definitely think he was a wimp. And his parents would be really disappointed in him and make him quit his job.

On the other hand, if he *did* do it, he would be able to keep his job, keep helping Spike, keep his parents happy *and* save his reputation in front of Luke.

133

Besides, he was positive he could get his marks back up again by January, when the next report cards came out.

"Okay," he said, sitting down in front of the typewriter.

Luke took over out front, and for the next hour, Shane worked on changing the three C's to B's. He didn't want to go too far by putting down A's. Besides, he was pretty sure his parents would be satisfied with a straight B report card.

At nine o'clock the boys were almost ready to leave. "Wanna go to a party?" Luke asked. He must have seen the look of surprise on Shane's face, because he said, "Hey, it was your first time last week. I did the same thing my first time. And tonight, we'll stay away from the rye."

"All right!" said Shane.

"We'll stop at the beer store again," said Luke.

"Sure," Shane replied, grabbing his coat. He wanted to get that feeling again, like he'd had after the beers last week. He'd felt so relaxed and happy.

"You got any money?" asked Luke nonchalantly. "I haven't forgotten what I owe you," he said quickly. "It's just I already spent this pay cheque."

Shane hesitated for a second, then said,

"Sure, I've got tons of money."

The next day Shane sat at the breakfast table with his parents, feeling hung over. He had to leave for work soon. He knew they had seen his report card, because he had left it out on the kitchen table the previous night, before stumbling to bed.

"We saw your report card, son," his dad started.

Shane looked down at the tablecloth and fiddled nervously with his eggs. He didn't think the card looked very professional, and his dad sounded grave. The little white lies he had been telling with more and more frequency were one thing; this was out-and-out deception.

"We know your marks aren't quite as good as they have been in the past," Mr. McKay continued.

Shane put down his fork. He was beginning to wish he had never let Luke talk him into doing it.

"... but considering how well you're doing at your job and considering how often you work, well, we're very proud of you, son."

Shane started to cough. His dad whacked him on the back. "You okay?"

"Yeah," Shane whispered. "Piece of bacon caught in my throat."

"We're pleased that you're showing so much responsibility, dear," his mom added. "With the number of hours you work every week, well, we were impressed that you could still manage all B's."

When Shane got to work, he told Luke what had happened. "All right!" said Luke, slapping him on the back. "Way to go." He walked away, laughing. "Parents! They're so gullible!"

Shane forced a smile. But he knew his parents weren't gullible; they trusted him. And he couldn't shake the sense of guilt he had been carrying with him since morning.

Luke came back from the storage fridge and threw Shane a Coke. "Congratulations," he said. "I'm kind of glad, you know. It would've been a bummer if you couldn't work here anymore." He took a swig of pop before he noticed Shane's silence. "You did the right thing. What are a few marks?"

Shane smiled, for real this time. Luke was right. He gave good advice, just like Chuck did.

It had been a sticky situation, but he had handled it. He started to whistle as he put the ketchup bottles on the tables.

"I can handle anything," he thought proudly.

CHAPTER 33

It was the last day of school before the Christmas holidays. Shane was sitting by himself in the cafeteria with a half-eaten tuna sandwich on the table in front of him. In his hand was a Christmas card.

It was from Chuck. Shane had written three letters to him since September, and this morning he finally received something back.

Hey, Splash, thanks for your letters. Sorry I haven't written till now, but it's like I told you before. I'm a great talker, but a lousy writer!

I'm glad everything's going better for you at home and stuff. But maybe you took some of my advice the wrong way? I don't know. I mean, you know me, I'm always spewing out

*garbage on one topic or another. Anyway, I
guess I just wanted to say Be Careful. I'm real
glad you're having fun, but this drinking and
smoking scene sounds kinda heavy. I don't
wanna lay any trips on you, buddy, but hey,
I just want you back at camp this summer!
You are still coming back to camp this summer, aren't you?*

*I've already got writer's cramp. Merry
Christmas, Splash, and write again. Your
pal, Chuck.*

Shane reread the card one more time, then
stuffed it into his pocket. He had thought
Chuck would be impressed with his new life-
style. Maybe his friend wasn't as cool as he
had thought.

Besides, he really enjoyed partying with
Luke. They hung around each other all the
time now. Shane didn't even try out for the
hockey team, because he knew if he did he
would have to give up most of his evenings
with Luke and some of his work shifts.

Shane knew his friendship with Luke was
lopsided. Luke was definitely the leader. He
made all the decisions on where they were
going, what they were going to do, and who
they were going to do it with. And, more
often than not, it was Shane who had to foot
the bill for their "party favours," Luke's ex-

pression for alcohol.

But Shane didn't really care if he had to pay for most of the booze. He liked to drink. He almost felt like he fit in with the other guys when he was drunk. He almost felt cool. Even Luke told him he was much more loose and fun when he was drunk.

Occasionally, Shane reflected on the fact that what he was doing was ridiculous, and that he should just be himself, but it was easy to push those thoughts from his mind. Being himself would mean having no friends again.

Besides, he was proud to hang around with Luke. There was always something to do. They didn't hang around BLT or Joey or Snake or any of the other Degrassi kids much anymore, because those guys didn't like to party the way Shane and Luke did. BLT said he thought their drinking was stupid. But Shane just thought BLT was immature. In fact, he couldn't believe he used to look up to any of them.

He told himself he didn't need any other friends at Degrassi, now that he was hanging out with Luke's high school friends. While kids like Joey were going to video parlours and movies on the weekends, Shane and Luke were going to wild drinking parties all the time. Sometimes, after they had all been drinking, they would pile into someone's parents' car and go driving. Shane knew this was stupid and dangerous, but he wasn't going to be the one to point it out. Besides, it was fun, living in the fast lane.

"Oh, look! Everybody, look!" Shane was roused from his daydreaming by Alexa's excited sing-song voice on the other side of the cafeteria. When the hum of voices got louder, he turned around to see what all the excitement was about.

To his surprise, he saw Spike walking toward her friends with Emma's bassinet in her arms. He moved a bit closer, and saw that Emma was *in* the bassinet.

"What's Emma doing here?" he heard Spike's friend Erica asked.

"The girl who takes care of her during the day — her dad had an accident," Spike replied. "He's okay. But she had to go see him. She couldn't stay with Emma."

A crowd formed immediately around Spike and the baby. Suddenly Shane wanted to tell them all not to get so close. She was only a little baby, after all. One of them might give her a cold, or some other weird infection.

But he kept his mouth shut. He knew he had no right to act fatherly all of a sudden. In the past two months, he had only seen

Emma twice. And it wasn't because Spike hadn't asked him over, either. Every time Shane gave her the weekly twenty dollars, Spike would ask if he wanted to come over and see the baby. But it seemed that every night she suggested it, he was either working or going out with Luke, until finally she stopped asking.

He supposed he was avoiding seeing Emma. After all, he told himself, he gave Spike twenty dollars a week. Eighty dollars a month! He was doing more than enough.

He was brought back to earth by Alexa's loud voice again. "She's so sweet!" she squealed.

"You should be around when she decides she doesn't want to go to sleep," Spike said with a laugh. "Then she isn't so sweet."

Shane picked up his binder and threw out his tuna sandwich; then he shuffled his way slowly over to the table and peered between the shoulders and heads of his classmates at Emma.

She lay so quietly in her bassinet, like a little Christmas angel. Her eyes were open and she looked around her, as if over-whelmed that all these people would be wanting to stare at *her*. It seemed to Shane that she caught his eye. She gave one of her little "gas smiles," as Spike called them, right in his direction. He pushed his way through the other students.

"Can I hold her?" he said abruptly.

Spike looked up, surprised. She hesitated for a moment, and Shane saw the glimmer in her eyes, as if she was deciding whether to blast him, or be nice to him.

Perhaps it was Christmas spirit that took over, or perhaps it was the fact that she knew he would be giving her another twenty dollars soon, because she said, "Okay. But only for a bit." The crowd parted, almost respectful of Shane, who was, after all, the father of this darling creature. He picked the baby up gently. He was surprised that he remembered how.

Everyone was staring at him, so he walked away to the other side of the cafeteria. "Hi, Emma," he whispered. "It's Daddy."

He sat down in a chair and rocked her slowly. She smiled at him. He kissed her soft little forehead. "I know I don't see you much," he whispered to her, "but it doesn't mean I don't love you a whole lot."

He continued to rock her, and her tiny blue eyes blinked once, twice, then stayed closed.

"I'm working hard, Emma," he whispered. "Who knows? Maybe one day me and Luke will have our own apartment together, and you can come over and visit."

The bell rang, signalling the end of lunch. Emma stayed asleep.

"Shane?"

He looked up and saw Spike standing over him. She was carrying the empty bassinet. "I have to take her with me to math," she said gently.

He stood up, moving close to Spike. They both gazed down at Emma. Shane thought that if someone took a picture right now, they'd look like a happy little family.

"Merry Christmas, Emma," he whispered. He gave her one last kiss and handed her back to Spike.

"How are things with you, Shane?" Spike asked, a hint of anxiousness in her voice.

"Fine. Great. Why?"

"Oh, you know," she said, almost apologetic. "Rumours."

"What do you mean?"

"Well ... that you and Luke drink. And do drugs."

Shane snorted. "I can't believe this! So what if we do? It's not like we're doing anything we can't handle."

Spike studied him for a moment. "You know, you sound more like Luke when you say that stuff than Shane McKay."

"Well, maybe Shane McKay has changed,"

he answered defensively.

"Okay, okay." Spike said. "Just be careful."

"Yes, Mom," he said, unable to suppress a grin. "Boy, you can sure tell you're a parent."

She smiled. "I guess you can."

"Anyway," he continued, "I'm independent."

Her smile faded. "You know, you've been throwing that word around a lot lately. But there's a difference between being independent and being an idiot."

"Spike! Give me a break!"

"I just think drinking and stuff is dumb."

"Don't worry about me, okay?" He looked at his watch. "You and Emma are late for math."

"Right," she smiled, looking down at Emma. "Come on, Em. Let's go learn our integers." They started to walk away.

"Spike?" he called after her. "Merry Christmas."

She turned around. "Merry Christmas to you, too, Shane."

CHAPTER 34

Shane trudged home from school, his boots sinking in the snow on the uncleared sidewalk. It was only four o'clock, but already it was almost dark. He hated winter, and it was only the end of January, which meant there were two long months left.

He felt better the minute he stepped into the house. At least it was Friday, and nobody was home yet. He went through the rooms switching on lights. Then he climbed the stairs to his room. He opened the bottom drawer of his desk. This was his secret drawer, because it even had a key, which he kept hidden in a box on his dresser. When he was a kid, he had used it to hide things like his favourite marbles, or stones that he imagined were gold. Now he used it for very different things.

He took his latest report card out of the drawer and examined it, swearing softly to himself. None of his marks had improved since November. In fact, he had one more C. But that wasn't the worst of it. He had received the report card on Monday, and on Tuesday he had tried to doctor it up at Joe's. But he hadn't let the liquid paper dry long enough, and he had ended up with a smudged B. It was useless now. There was no way he could give it to his parents.

His parents had started asking him when he would get his report card. They knew it was due about now. And his homeroom teacher, Mr. Garcia, was beginning to wonder why Shane hadn't returned a copy with his parents' signatures.

Finally, Shane told him he had lost it. Mr. Garcia was kind enough to tell him he would get him a copy. But it would only be a copy — one that Shane couldn't doctor.

Shane tried to look on the bright side. If he acted ashamed and surprised at his marks, and promised to stay in one night every weekend to study, maybe his parents wouldn't be so mad.

He put the card back. There were only two other items in the drawer: his weekly finance sheet and a small bag of marijuana.

He had bought it with Luke one day about

a month ago, from one of Luke's high school friends, Mike. Shane was surprised the first time he met Mike. He had expected a guy with long greasy hair and wild eyes. Instead, he'd stood face to face with a clean-cut boy who wore an expensive leather jacket and a polo shirt.

He didn't really like Mike, but Luke did, so Shane kept his mouth shut. They didn't have to see him very often; just at parties, or when Luke wanted a bit of hash or pot. Usually Shane didn't buy anything for himself, but sometimes he had to lend Luke the money to get his. And one day Luke had pressured him into it, saying Shane always smoked *his* stuff.

That wasn't really true. Whenever Luke lit up a joint, Shane would take the smallest tokes possible. He wouldn't refuse, because he didn't want Luke to accuse him of being a wimp. But he never got very stoned. He didn't like the feeling it gave him.

Drinking was different, though. He liked drinking beer, a lot. When he drank beer, he always felt like a more interesting and fun person. A fair amount of his money went to beer.

"Hi, dear."

Shane jumped. He kicked the drawer closed with his foot as he looked toward his bedroom door. "Oh, uh, hi, Mom. How was your day?"

"Oh, fine. I gave blood this morning, and this afternoon I was at the Christian Women's Association. We're trying to figure out some way to raise awareness in kids about the dangers of drugs, through the church. Without being preachy."

Shane smiled weakly.

"Any suggestions?"

"Huh? Uh … no."

"Of course. Why would you have suggestions? You've never been influenced by things like that, anyway."

Shane forced a smile. "Let's go downstairs. I'm starving. I need a snack."

As they started to leave the room, his mom looked at his T-shirt. "What does it mean?" she asked, pointing at the shirt.

"It's the name of a band."

"*The Gourmet Scum*?? What kind of a name is that?"

Shane couldn't help laughing. "It's just a name, Mom."

"I suppose so. Makes me feel old, though. When I was young, the names were so simple. 'The Four Lads,' 'The Duke Ellington Band.'" They continued down the stairs. "Are you going out tonight?"

"Yeah. Just over to Luke's."

"He seems nice enough. Quiet. You should have him over for dinner one night."

Somehow, Shane couldn't picture his mom, dad, him and Luke sitting around the dining room table. He could just imagine the expression on Luke's face when his dad started to say grace.

They reached the kitchen and Shane went to the fridge. "I might stay overnight there," he said, "since I have to work the Saturday shift, too."

"Fine. As long as you're home in time for church on Sunday."

Shane smiled. His parents didn't even ask questions anymore when he asked if he could stay at Luke's.

"By the way, when is your report card coming out?"

"Monday," said Shane. "I just found out today."

"Bit late this year."

"Really? I can't remember."

After dinner, he went back up to his room to get a change of clothes and some money to take to Luke's. He couldn't get rid of a nagging sense of guilt about his report card. It bothered him that after all this time, he still felt guilty about things like this. But he sometimes felt that his lies to his parents were accumulating at such a rapid pace, he was going to start drowning.

"Drowning in a sea of lies," he muttered to himself. "*Now* I think of a metaphor! Why couldn't I have thought of it on the English exam? Oh, well, in a few hours I'll be drowning myself in a sea of beer instead."

He laughed as he left the room. He didn't notice that he had forgotten to lock the bottom drawer of his desk.

CHAPTER 35

Shane arrived home Sunday morning. He hadn't spoken with his parents since Friday evening, when he had left for Luke's. He dragged himself into the house. His head was pounding from all the beer he had consumed, and he was still trying to come up with a good excuse to get out of going to church. He just wanted to crawl into his bed and pass out.

"Shane." He heard his father's voice from the kitchen. "Come in here. Right now."

Shane walked into the kitchen. His parents sat at the table. They looked awful. They hadn't looked that way since — Shane racked his brain for a second — since he'd told them about Spike.

"What's wrong?" A terrible thought hit him. The baby. Something had happened to

Emma.

Then he looked down at the kitchen table. Everything from his bottom drawer — the pot, his finance sheets and his report card — lay on the table.

His knees grew weak.

"Sit down," his dad said slowly.

Shane kept standing, not because he wanted to disobey his father, but because he was in a daze. Suddenly, Mr. McKay stood up, grabbed his son and shoved him into a chair. Shane was surprised at how strong his father was. His grip hurt. "Sit down!" he screamed, even though Shane was already seated.

"I can explain ..."

"Please try," his dad said sadly. "Please try."

But Shane couldn't think of anything. For the first time in a long while, he couldn't come up with a single lie.

"Okay ... the pot. I never use it. I swear. I bought it because Luke does it, and I guess I ... I wanted to fit in."

He glanced at his parents, trying to gauge their response. But they sat with their heads lowered. He continued. "The report card. When I saw my marks, I was afraid you'd make me quit my job. So I tried to change it. Then I realized I was being stupid, so ... I told Mr. Garcia I'd lost it, and he was going to give me a new one on Monday. Which I was going to give you as is."

"Oh, Shane," his mother sighed. "Why get yourself into more trouble? We talked to Mr. Garcia. He told us your marks were almost as bad in November. The school checked that report card. I can't believe we didn't notice you'd changed it then, but … "

"Why the hell would we notice?" his father cut in. "For some crazy reason, your mother and I thought we could finally trust you!"

"You can … "

"Stop it! Just stop it," said Mr. McKay. "You've been pulling the wool over our eyes all year. You must think we're old fools."

Shane felt a lump forming in his throat. "No, I don't! I just didn't want to hurt you any more than I already have, that's all," he blurted out. "I know it was wrong … but everything finally seemed okay. I didn't want to ruin things again."

"It's too late," said his mom quietly.

"And this!" his dad waved the finance sheet in front of his face. "Twenty dollars a week to Spike. I could have overlooked that, son. After all, it is your money. But twelve dollars a week on beer?" He threw the sheet on the table in disgust.

"We're sending you to private school,

Shane," Mrs. McKay said. "We mean it this time."

His mouth dropped open.

"You start there in two weeks," his mother continued. "We couldn't get you in any earlier."

Two weeks! Shane's mind was racing. "But ... why bother ... why bother spending the money for only a few months? Why not ground me, instead?"

"Don't you see, Shane?" his mom said wearily. "Your father and I are at our wits' end. It's not even a matter of punishment. We just don't know how to handle you."

Shane was silent for a moment. Then he said quietly, "But I can handle myself."

His father slammed his fist down on the table. "For God's sake!" he yelled. "*Listen* to what you're saying!"

"It's not easy, raising a teenager at our age," his mom added. "But I really thought we were starting to do okay." Her voice cracked, and Shane saw the tears start to stream down her face.

"I swear I didn't mean to hurt you," he whispered.

"No," his father corrected him. "You didn't ever mean for us to *find out*. You don't give a damn about our feelings."

"Look, I know I made a few mistakes ... "

His mother looked at him, her eyes wide. "Don't you see, Shane? It isn't just a few mistakes. You've ended up completely on the wrong track."

"In whose opinion?"

"Ours, the school's ..."

"Right," he snorted. "So, in the adults' opinions."

"No, Shane. In the opinions of the people who care about you."

"You don't care about me!" he cried out. "Or why would you be sending me away?"

His father spoke again, in a tired voice. "Because we've tried to guide you. And we haven't succeeded. You need some guidance, son."

"I don't *need* anything!" he shouted, feeling tears stinging his eyes. "I definitely don't need private school. And I definitely don't need you!"

He felt like he was watching the perfect little world he had built for himself crumble around his feet. The tears started rolling down his face, and he ran out of the room.

CHAPTER 36

"Look at it this way," Luke was saying. "You've got about ten days left of absolute freedom."

"Yeah, sure." Shane took another swig of beer, but even beer didn't make him feel good tonight.

They were in Luke's room. It was Friday night, after work. And it was Shane's fifteenth birthday. His parents had acknowledged it with a card and a sweater his mother had knit. They had wanted to celebrate when Shane got home from work, but he'd told them curtly that he had other plans.

So this was his celebration. He and Luke were listening to loud music and getting drunk, as usual.

Shane had barely said a word to his

parents since their argument a week before. He had tried to think up ways to get out of going to private school but, short of running away, he couldn't think of anything.

So he had decided that the least he could do was make his parents' lives as miserable as they had made his. And it was working. His mom cried almost constantly, and his father looked like he wasn't sleeping.

Deep down, he knew he was being cruel. But he was completely absorbed in his own pain. He could only think of himself.

He seldom went home, he never told his parents where he was going, and he got drunk almost every night. Once, the police had come to Luke's house because his parents were frantic about his whereabouts. Luke hadn't appreciated it. He had thought he was getting busted.

"Hey, man, don't look so bummed out," said Luke. He threw Shane another beer. But Shane was already drunk. His reaction was a split second too slow, and the beer can rolled onto the floor. He picked it up and cracked it open, the foam squirting him in the face. Luke laughed. Shane didn't.

Luke's smile faded. "Listen, man, no offense, but ... you're being a drag."

"Sorry," Shane replied. He was grateful to Luke for letting him hang out at his place,

but he could see that Luke was already drift-
ing away from him. After all, he had lots of
friends. The only thing he'd miss about
Shane would be his money. Luke had
bummed plenty of money off him in the past
few months.

But despite that, Shane was going to miss
Luke, a lot. Luke was his only friend. He was
also the only person at school who knew Shane
was leaving. Shane didn't see the point in telling everyone. He thought it would be interesting to imagine what they'd think a week from
now, when he wasn't there. But then, maybe
nobody would even notice.

He knew he had to tell Spike. His last shift
had been tonight, which meant only one
more child support payment. His parents
were going to give him his ten dollars' allowance a week again, so he could give her
half of that. But it would hardly be the same.
He knew she'd been saving all the money he
gave her for things Emma needed. Five dollars a week seemed like an insult.

"Man, you're wasted!" He heard Luke
laughing on the other side of the room.
Shane stretched out on the old plaid couch
that had become his bed, and closed his eyes.
He knew he would pass out quickly.

As he drifted off to sleep, he wished he
would never wake up.

CHAPTER 37

Spike took the news well. "Oh, no," she said quietly. The two of them were hunched together at a table in the cafeteria. "That's awful. I'm sorry."

Shane leaned back in his chair and sighed. He thought it was strange that despite all the hard and rotten times they had had, Spike was always the one who understood best when things were at their worst for him.

"I just feel really bad about the money ... " he started.

"Forget it. It's not like you did it on purpose." She started to laugh. "Isn't it strange how you sometimes do all these things because you really believe at the time that it's the right thing to do, and then it turns out to be the biggest mistake you ever made?"

Shane realized he was shaking. "It's so

good to talk to you," he said. The only other person he'd talked to was Luke, who got bored quickly with what he called Shane's "sob stories."

"So, this week will be the last time I can pay you. After that, it'll be back to five dollars a week."

Spike shrugged. "Hey, five bucks a week is still something. And I'm going to get a full-time job this summer."

"I guess I'll be back at camp this summer. I'll be a regular counsellor this year. The money isn't great, but I'll be able to send you most of it. It isn't like there's anything to spend it on up there."

He realized Spike was staring at him, a sad expression on her face. "You know what?" She sounded surprised. "I'm going to miss you." She leaned over and kissed him.

Shane dug his fingernails into his palms. "I'm going to miss you, too. And Emma. I know I haven't visited her as much as I should, but ... anyway, I'm going to miss both of you a lot."

Spike stood up. "Speaking of Emma," she said apologetically, "I've got to call her sitter. She's had a bad cold the past few days."

"Spike? Could I come visit her? Before I leave?"

"Of course you can. Any time."

As he watched her walk away, he felt tears spring up in his eyes for a moment, but he bit his lower lip hard and swallowed. Then he got up and walked out of the cafeteria.

CHAPTER 38

"Man, Gourmet Scum's breaking up after this tour. It's the last chance you'll ever get to see them."

Luke stood by Shane's locker, watching him sort through the piles of junk that had accumulated over the year. It was Tuesday, and he had four more days left at Degrassi Junior High. He didn't know why he was already cleaning out his locker, but he thought it might be easier to do it bit by bit throughout the week.

"Sorry," Shane replied. "I'd really like to go. But Spike counts on that money."

Luke rolled his eyes. "So just once you don't pay her. It won't make any difference."

"But this is the last time I can give her twenty bucks." Shane fingered the twenty dollars in his pocket.

"All the better," Luke said. "She must already be getting used to the idea that she won't be seeing all that cash anymore."

Shane didn't say anything. He examined a dirty, wrinkled pair of socks that had lodged themselves into a crevice at the bottom of his locker. So that was what he had been smelling since October. He threw them into the garbage.

"It's your last weekend in Toronto," Luke said. "You've got to go out with a bang."

Shane thought about what Luke was saying. It would be nice to go out with a bang. His parents were driving him up to Strathcona on Sunday, and the concert was Saturday night. Everyone he knew was going. If he didn't go to the concert, he would have to sit at home all night with his parents.

"I don't suppose you could ... uh ... lend me the money?" he asked. Luke had "borrowed" over a hundred dollars from Shane since he had started working at Joe's, and so far he hadn't paid back a penny.

"Sorry," Luke said guiltily. "I'm almost broke myself. Got just enough for one ticket. I'll pay you back what I owe you, though, honest," he said quickly. "I'll mail it to your new school."

Shane stared at Luke. Luke tried to hold his gaze, but finally he looked down at the floor. They both knew he would never pay Shane back.

"You'll love it at the concert," he continued quickly. "Everyone talks and makes jokes, even though they don't know each other. Man, it's like one big party."

Shane was listening intently now. Perhaps that's what he needed. A big party before leaving for dumb, boring private school.

After all, he had given Spike about three hundred dollars already. That was a lot of money from someone who had just turned fifteen.

"Tell you what," said Luke. "You come up with the money for the ticket, and I'll supply the party favours."

Shane's eyes lit up. "You'll get some beer?"

"Better than beer."

"Hash? Pot?"

"Better than hash or pot."

"What?"

"Acid."

"Acid? I don't know ... "

"You've gotta try it. Just as an experiment. Everyone does it at a concert."

"Yeah? You've done it before?"

"Sure. Lots of times."

Shane tried to busy himself with his locker cleanout.

"Look, I'm just telling you," said Luke. "I'm gonna get some anyway. From Mike. It's up to you if you want to do it or not. But if you want to ... it'll be like my going away present to you."

With that, Luke started to walk away. Shane stood rooted to the spot, doing some fast thinking.

"Hey, Luke!" he shouted. Luke turned around. "Here." He reached into his pocket and handed Luke the twenty dollars that was supposed to go to Spike. "Get me a ticket."

Luke's face lit up. "Great! You won't regret it, man. This is going to be one amazing evening."

As Luke continued down the hall, Shane turned back to the mess in his locker, smiling. After all, it *was* his money, and he should have fun his last night in town.

Now all he had to do was tell Spike.

CHAPTER 39

He told her on Wednesday. "I, uh, didn't get my pay cheque like I thought I would," he lied. "Joe's mailing it to me up at Strathcona."

Spike's face fell. "Oh, well," she said, trying not to sound disappointed, "it's not your fault. I'll just have to wait a bit longer to get Emma her new snowsuit. She grows so fast!"

As he walked away, Shane felt like a big schmuck. Yet he could hardly go back and tell her the truth, particularly since Luke had already bought his ticket.

But somehow she found out the truth on her own. Shane didn't know why this surprised him so much. Gossip spread at Degrassi faster than fire.

On Friday afternoon, he was conspiring

with Luke in the library.

"Did you get the stuff?" he whispered.

"No. I couldn't find Mike. But I know he'll be at the concert. He always hangs around outside the Gardens before a concert."

"So … what's it like?" Shane had been thinking about it all week. He was still pretty nervous, and hadn't made up his mind whether or not to do it.

"It's incredible, man. It takes about a half hour before you feel anything. Then you start to take off. In a couple of hours, you peak. Then you're flying."

"Yeah? All right!" He couldn't imagine anything that could make him feel that good, particularly the way he'd been feeling the past couple of weeks. Beer didn't make him feel like a better person anymore; maybe acid would.

"What a great way to spend my last night here!" he said.

"Shane." He turned around. Spike suddenly was standing behind him, and she didn't look pleased. "You liar," she said, her voice rising. "You said you couldn't give me the money because you didn't get paid."

People's heads were turning in their direction. Shane thought the last thing he needed on his final day at Degrassi was another scene.

167

"Spike," he said in a low voice, hoping her voice would lower with his.

But it didn't. "If you didn't get paid, how can you afford a twenty-dollar concert ticket?"

Shane felt his face getting hot. He knew he was blushing. He looked at Luke, who was shaking his head.

"Well, why shouldn't I? I'm entitled to a life. And it's my money."

"Then why couldn't you just be honest for a change? Instead of telling another stupid lie!"

Everyone was watching them now, even the librarian, Ms. Baxter. Shane wished she would tell Spike to keep it down, but for some reason, she seemed to be glued to her seat. He wished he could make himself disappear.

"You don't give a damn about me, or Emma," Spike snapped.

"That's not true."

"Forget about coming to see her before you go. Forget about ever seeing her again."

"Spike!" he pleaded.

"You know, I really thought you'd changed, but you haven't. You walk around acting like you're Mr. Cool, Mr. Mature," she ranted, "but underneath your little façade you're still a *pig*." She spat out the last word. Then she turned on her heels and stormed out of the library.

There was dead silence. Even Luke didn't say anything. Finally Ms. Baxter found her voice. "Okay, everyone, back to work."

Slowly the other kids went back to their work. He heard someone snicker. Shane felt himself begin to tremble.

He got up and walked out of the library. He still had two classes to go to that afternoon, but what was the point?

He walked out of Degrassi and down the front steps. When he reached the sidewalk, he turned. "Bye forever," he said to the red brick exterior.

CHAPTER 40

The night of the concert, Shane dressed carefully. He put on his favourite band T-shirt, then changed it in favour of one of his own tie-dye creations. As he looked through all the new clothes he had acquired over the year, he realized he wouldn't get to wear them very often at Strathcona. As of Monday, he would be wearing burgundy pants, a burgundy blazer, a white button-down shirt and a navy tie.

He chuckled bitterly, thinking that a year ago it wouldn't have bothered him so much. A year ago, he had worn clothes that were almost that bad. But now that he finally had what he liked to think of as his own style, he had to start dressing exactly like everyone else.

Eventually he settled on his blue, purple

and green tie-dye shirt. It was unusually mild for February, so he threw on his old jean jacket and put on his ski vest over top.

He looked at his watch. Time to go. He was meeting Luke and a few other guys outside the Gardens in half an hour.

At the dinner table his mother had asked if he was going out on his last night in town.

"Yeah."

"Where?"

"Just out."

His parents had looked at each other. But all his father said was, "Just make sure you're home by one o'clock tomorrow. I should be home from church by then, and we'll leave for Strathcona right away."

Shane made a mental note not to come home before two.

"Do you have your things packed?" his mom had asked, concerned.

"Almost," said Shane.

"Need any help?"

"No."

Now, as he descended the stairs, he heard his mother talking quietly on the phone. "We love Shane so much, Stephanie," she was saying to her best friend, "but I truly believe private school will do him good. It'll probably do Steven some good, too. I've been so worried about his health lately. He thinks everything that's happened is his fault. He's no spring chicken, you know. It might do him some good to have Shane away for a while."

Shane took the rest of the steps two at a time, landing as hard as he could. Then he ran out the front door, slamming it hard behind him. He wanted his mother to know he had heard every word.

CHAPTER 41

"Wow," Shane thought as he emerged from the subway. He had never been to a rock concert before. Now here he was, still a block from the arena, and he was surrounded by other kids all heading to the concert. Everyone was in a good mood, and howls of "Parteeee!" and "Whoooo!" echoed through the air.

Luke was right, he thought, as he let the crowd carry him along. This *was* going to be one big party.

He rounded the corner and immediately saw Luke talking with Mike. He hung back, not wanting to talk to Mike, and not wanting Luke to ask him for money at the last minute. He only had enough for the subway home.

But Mike was walking away, and Luke

spotted Shane. They walked toward each other and, acting as nonchalant as he could, Luke placed something in Shane's palm.

"Acid!" Shane said, a little too loud.

Luke rolled his eyes. "Don't be an idiot, man. Put it away."

Another guy from school, Tim, approached them. "Hi, guys," he said. Tim was a nice, smart black kid in their grade. Shane knew this was his first concert, too, which made him feel better. But, unlike Shane, Tim hadn't been embarrassed to admit it.

Shane's curiosity was killing him. He opened his hand and looked down at two little pieces of paper. "I thought it would be a pill."

Tim's eyes widened. "Drugs?" Neither Shane nor Luke answered him. "You guys doing drugs?"

Shane wasn't sure why, but suddenly he felt proud of the fact that he and Luke were in on this together.

"So, how do you take it?" he said, a bit cocky.

"Just swallow it."

"You eat paper?" Suddenly Shane didn't feel so cool anymore.

Luke was getting fed up with him. "Hey," he said, looking right at him, "if you can't eat paper, maybe you're not ready for acid."

Tim piped up. "You guys are crazy. That stuff's dangerous."

"Yeah, yeah, yeah," replied Luke.

Shane looked at the piece of paper in his hand. How could such a tiny thing be dangerous?

"They mix LSD with strychnine, so the acid stays in your body. You know what strychnine is?" asked Tim.

Shane looked at Luke, who shook his head, uninterested.

"Rat poison. It kills rats, really painfully. It can kill humans, too."

Shane tried to laugh, but it sounded forced. "Uh ... hey, Luke, maybe this isn't such a good idea."

"Relax," Luke said. "I've done acid before, and I'm okay." With that, he put both pieces of paper in his mouth and swallowed. He seemed to be reading Shane's thoughts, be- cause he said, "You don't have to eat it if you don't want to." He didn't say it very sincere- ly, though.

Shane looked from Tim to Luke. "I'm not chicken," he replied. But he didn't put the paper in his mouth right away. He looked at the two pieces sitting in his hand.

"You should only take one," Luke said, "since it's your first time. You can save the other piece for a rainy day."

Shane popped one in his mouth and swallowed. It was so easy! He looked at the other one in his hand for a moment, then said, "What the hell," and popped it in, too.

Luke stared at him. Then he started to laugh. "Boy, are you ever gonna fly tonight!"

Tim just shook his head. At that moment they were joined by a few other guys from school. Joey was there, and Snake. BLT, Lucy and a few other kids were close behind.

"Okay!" Joey shouted. "Are we ready?"

Luke caught Shane's eye and smiled. "We sure are!"

"Okay! Party time!"

They all headed into the concert, chanting, "Scum, Scum, here we come!" Shane started chanting with them, smiling broadly. This was going to be great.

CHAPTER 42

The Gourmet Scum hadn't started yet. The crowd was getting restless, and people were beginning to clap loudly and hold their lighters above their heads. Hundreds of flames glimmered in the darkness of the stadium.

Shane was starting to feel disappointed. He looked over at Luke, who had a huge grin on his face. "It's been a half hour," Shane told him in a low voice, "and I don't feel a thing."

Luke seemed to think this was hysterical. He looked Shane in the face and started to laugh uncontrollably. "You'll ... you'll feel it any minute, man. I promise. You probably ate a huge dinner." He stared at Shane's face for a while and started to laugh again. "You look so funny!" he howled.

"I do? What do you mean? How come?"

"*Everyone* looks funny."

Suddenly a roar came up from the crowd. Shane looked toward the stage, which seemed to be about a mile away from where they sat. He realized the ant-like figures moving across the stage had to be the Gourmet Scum. He started to cheer too.

Then, the moment they started their first song, it hit him like a slap in the face.

He looked around at the people he was with. Their faces looked unreal, overdone and distorted out of shape. He could barely hear the music. The instruments seemed to blend together.

He fell back down into his chair, sweating and not moving, for about twenty minutes.

"You okay?" he heard Joey ask.

"Yeah ... fine ... I'm fine."

Luke bent down. "You'll be okay in a few minutes," he shouted. "It's always pretty weird the first little bit."

Shane grinned tensely and didn't budge from his seat.

Another ten minutes passed, then he dared to stand up again and look around.

His friends' faces still looked ghostly, sort of green in colour. But it didn't scare him anymore. Now it seemed incredibly funny. He started to laugh. Just watching the people in the crowd was a great show in itself.

He watched one guy sing along to the

lyrics. His mouth seemed all twisted out of shape as he sang. Shane thought he looked like a big chimpanzee. He started to laugh even harder.

Then he turned toward the stage. Suddenly he became aware of the sound. It was amazing. It was the best music he had ever heard. But he wasn't just hearing it, he was feeling it. It pounded through his body. The bass line felt like it was flowing through his veins along with his blood.

He watched the band members and, as he stared, the whole stage became a series of purple and green cubes. Even the musicians were made of cubes. It was beautiful. He kept staring, wanting the image to last. He had an overwhelming desire to get closer to the stage. Everyone was so wrapped up in the concert that nobody saw him leave his seat.

He felt sure of himself as he walked toward the stage, but he didn't get very far. As soon as he tried to hop over to the next level of seats, a huge bouncer stopped him. Shane was sure he had never seen anyone as big as this man, so he didn't try to argue, but moved off to the side.

He hadn't felt this confident and happy in a long time. As he stood watching the band, he felt that everything was moving in slow motion. He wanted the night to last forever.

CHAPTER 43

Shane was standing on an old bridge, looking down into a valley below. He supposed
that a long time ago, a river must have
flowed under the bridge. But it was all dried
up now.

He was still high as a kite. He wasn't sure
where he was. He had lost his friends long
ago, and had been wandering aimlessly ever
since.

Suddenly a horrible thought hit him. Had
Luke and the others lost him on purpose?
Maybe Luke thought he acted too stupid on
acid, and he had told the other people they
were with. Maybe they were together somewhere right now, having a great time and
laughing about him.

Then he vaguely remembered that he was
the one who had split from his friends, and

he felt better. His heart stopped beating so fast, and he started to relax again.

Soon he would try to figure out where he was, he decided. Then he could make it to Luke's house. But for now he wanted to be outside, enjoying the sights and sounds. Everything seemed so much bigger and more beautiful on acid. Even an old tin can that Shane had kicked all the way from the arena was beautiful.

Shane looked down at the tin can. He brought his foot back, then kicked the can as hard as he could. It flew over the side of the bridge. He watched as it fell to the valley below. It didn't seem to fall, though; it seemed to soar through the air, not too fast, then land gracefully on the ground.

He bet he could do that, too. For the first time in his life, he felt he could do anything. If he just stood up on the edge of the rail and flapped his arms, he bet he could fly. Imagine if he could fly away from Toronto, far away to another country, to a new life! He wouldn't have to go to boarding school, and his parents would never have to worry about him again. Spike would be free to lead her own life with Emma.

They all hated him. Even Emma would probably grow up to hate him. She would hear bad stories from her mother, and Shane wouldn't be around to defend himself. If they ever did happen to meet, later in life, he could just imagine the hatred and disgust that would fill her eyes.

He didn't even have any friends! Luke wasn't a real friend, and Chuck was miles and miles away, and everyone at school thought he was a jerk.

"I *am* a jerk!" he laughed out loud. "I've screwed up."

He stood looking down into the valley. No matter what he did, it turned out bad. He supposed he was just one of those people who was destined to be a black sheep, a constant trouble-maker.

He started to laugh, and he heard it echo down in the valley below.

"Most people have no problem making people like them. But not me. I don't need them, anyway!" he shouted down into the valley. "I don't need anyone!"

He climbed up onto the railing of the bridge, gripping a support girder with one hand. He swung himself forward, enjoying the sensation.

"Private school," he muttered angrily. Gross. Where they strip you of your individuality and turn you into a robot.

Then he laughed again. Why should *he* care about individuality? Every time he tried to act like an individual, he only wound up making all the people he cared about, hate him.

Including himself.

Suddenly he was overcome with fear. He was in a trap, and he had to get out.

He looked down. It was quite a drop. He lost his balance and grabbed onto the steel girder.

For a few minutes he just stood there, trying to calm himself. It was quite cold now, but he didn't feel it.

A small bird flew in front of him, and he watched it, mesmerized. She made it look so easy! She was so free.

He let go of the girder. Bending his knees slightly, he started to slowly move his arms up and down, like he had seen the bird do with her wings. Then a gust of wind came along, pushing at his back. Shane lost his balance. Terrified, he reached out for the steel girder again.

But it was too late.

He was flying.

CHAPTER 44

For a long time there was nothing but darkness.

Then he started to dream.

The dream came in fragments, but the fragments were played back again and again.

He was in a white room. Everything was white. Even the people who came in and out of the room were in white. They seemed to float, they were so quiet. It was very peaceful.

People he knew started to enter his dream room. His parents were there. They never seemed to leave. Sometimes Carl was there. And Spike was in his dream, too. Sometimes different kids from school were there. Once he thought he saw Chuck.

It was a nice dream. He could feel love and

tenderness flowing from these people, and it was directed toward him.

After a while, the dream started to change. It had always been a silent dream, like a silent movie. But gradually the sound was being mixed in. The voices ran in circles around his brain, like a tape loop that couldn't be shut off. He heard many unfamiliar voices coming from the mysterious people in white. But mingled with the strange voices were familiar ones.

He was sure he heard his father's voice. "Shane ... Shane, please ... we love you so much ..."

"... Steven, please. Go home. I'll stay ..."

"... Everyone at school misses him ..."

"... Two weeks in a coma ..."

A coma! The word jolted Shane. He searched in vain for memories in every foggy corner of his brain, but it made him so tired .... He drifted back to sleep.

Then he remembered. He had been floating for a long time in this sleep that seemed to be somewhere between life and death, and it was quiet, easy and peaceful.

But now that he could remember, the peace was shattered. He remembered the baby; he remembered the quarrels with his parents and Spike; he remembered Luke and their many nights of drinking; he remembered the acid. He remembered everything. It was like someone had just handed him a collage depicting the last two years of his life.

Oh, God. The collage depressed him. Particularly when he got to the last image. He was watching himself fall, losing his balance on the bridge and plummeting to the hard ground below. "Why did I do that?" he chastised himself. "I could have died!"

His horror grew. "Maybe that's what I was trying to do. Maybe I was trying to die."

Shane felt frightened. "Do you want to die?"

Silence filled his head. Then, suddenly, a resounding "No!" echoed in his brain, loud and forceful.

"No," he said again. "I don't. I want a second chance."

"... son, can you hear me ..."

"Will you say a prayer for him? ..."

"Of course ..."

He wished he could wake up. He wanted to know where he was, if these voices were real or not.

But he was scared, too. He wondered how badly he had hurt himself. Would he be able to walk again? Play basketball? Go to school? He wanted answers, even though he knew he might not like what he heard.

He felt sluggish, like he had when he was a little boy with an awful fever. He would fall into fitful sleeps that seemed impossible to wake from. That's what it felt like now. He kept dreaming that he was awake and talking to the people around him; then he realized it was still part of his dream, and that he hadn't talked at all.

Then, one day it wasn't a dream. Someone was pinching him. Hard. He was vaguely aware that this wasn't the first time someone had pinched him in an attempt to wake him, but this was the first time it really hurt.

He tried to knock the hand away. When that didn't work, he tried to yell.

"Ow!" the voice sounded foreign to him. But it was his voice. Then he was aware of blurry shapes standing over him. He was awake!

He knew he had a long battle ahead of him. But for the moment that didn't concern him. Only one thing mattered for now.

Shane had opened his eyes.

About the Author

Susin Nielsen was born in 1964 and lives in Toronto, Ontario, with two fat cats. She graduated from Ryerson's Radio and Television Arts program in 1985.

For the past two years, Susin has spent most of her time as a script writer for the TV series *Degrssi Junior High,* and occasionally makes guest appearances on the show as the janitor, Louella. When not working, she explores the film and music scenes in Toronto, reads voraciously, studies Swedish and travels extensively. She wrote *Shane* while on a three-month trip to Stockholm, Sweden.

Look for Other Degrassi Books